Asian Indian Americans

FOOTSTEPS TO
AmericA

Asian Indian Americans

by Alexandra Bandon

New Discovery Books
Parsippany, New Jersey

ACKNOWLEDGMENT

Special thanks to the immigrants who shared their personal stories. Their names have been changed to protect their privacy.

PHOTO CREDITS

Front cover: Mary Ellen Matthews; Front and back cover (flag photo): Richard Bachmann
Mary Ellen Matthews: 9, 47, 50, 52, 73, 80, 82, 87, 90, 93, 96, 99, 102, 107
UPI/Bettmann: 12, 36
AP/Wide World Photos: 20, 30, 40, 64, 85,
Reuters/Bettmann: 23, 25

Published by New Discovery Books, an imprint of Silver Burdett Press.
A Simon & Schuster Company
299 Jefferson Road, Parsippany, NJ 07054
Printed in the United States of America
10 9 8 7 6 5 4 3 2 1

LIBRARY OF CONGRESS CATALOGING–IN–PUBLICATION DATA
Bandon, Alexandra.
Asian Indian Americans / by Alexandra Bandon. — 1st ed.
p.   cm. — (Footsteps to America)
Includes bibliographical references (p.   ) and index.
ISBN 0-02-768144-0
1. Indians of North American—Asian influences—Juvenile literature.
I. Title. II. Series.
E98.A84B36   1995
973'.0497—dc20   94-41698

Contents

Part I
The Land They Left Behind

= 1 =

Why Do They Leave?

The Land Shortage

Asian Indians are currently the fastest growing immigrant group coming to the United States, primarily because of liberal changes in immigration laws. But Asian Indian Americans (so called to distinguish them from Native American Indians) can trace their roots back to the turn of the twentieth century, when farmers from the north Indian state of Punjab came seeking their fortunes and new lands.

India is a country in southern Asia, bordered by Pakistan and China to the north and the Indian Ocean to the south. It is divided into many states, whose borders reflect the language divisions among the Asian Indian people. In 1858, India became part of the British Empire, solidifying the hold Britain's East India Company had over South Asia for centuries. By 1876, Queen Victoria added the title of "Empress of India" to her titles. Britain's imperial control over India was at its height. The colonial government, hoping to profit from Indian agriculture, imposed taxes on landowners. Small farmers in some of the northern states, such as Punjab, were forced to mortgage their lands at very high interest rates or sell them off at meager prices in order to pay the taxes. To make matters worse, most of the farmers in Punjab were Sikhs, a religious minority in India that was often in conflict with the British government and the Hindu religious majority.

For many years in agricultural states like Punjab, Bengal, and Gujarat, farmers had been dividing their lands among all their sons. But this constant division eventually turned large tracts of land into small, unprofitable plots. The farming conditions in Punjab only worsened in the later decades of the nineteenth century. A population explosion intensified the problems of dividing land, while droughts leading to famines and disease put a greater strain on the farmers' ability to make a profit.

Government construction of irrigation canals after 1900 eased the situation, but most northern Indians believed the fastest solution to the growing impoverishment of their villages could be found in encouraging younger sons to leave India and seek their fortunes elsewhere. These emigrants hoped to work for a few years and return to India with money to help support their extend-

Asian Indian Americans, found in almost any part of the United States, continue a pattern of immigration that dates to the early 1900s.

ed families. And their absence would mean less overcrowding in the villages.

By the early 1900s, thousands of Indians were leaving Punjab and other northern states for Australia, Africa, the Caribbean, and North America. A number of them headed for Canada, but instead eventually ended up in Washington State and California.

When people leave their country, they are called emigrants, but when they arrive at their destination they are immigrants (leaving a country permanently is emigrating; entering a country permanently is immigrating; moving around temporarily is migrating). Indians who come to the United States are known as Asian Indian immigrants or Asian Indian Americans. They are also known as first-generation Asian Indian Americans, and their American-born children would be called second-generation Asian Indian Americans. Asian Indian immigrants are often grouped with other Asian Americans, such as Korean Americans, Chinese Americans, Japanese Americans, or Vietnamese Americans.

The Restrictions

Asian Indian migration to the United States proved to be short lived at the turn of the century, however, because of a 1917 law that prohibited immigration from certain Asian countries. By the 1920s the flow to Washington State and California from Punjab had stopped, and those few Asian Indians living there found themselves in a predicament. Almost all the Asian Indians living on the West Coast in the 1910s and 1920s were men;

because the immigrants had seen themselves as sojourners, or temporary travelers, they had left their wives and families behind. Now they were in danger of not being allowed to return to the United States if they left to visit their families or bring back their wives. Some decided to return to India permanently, but most endured a life in the United States without their Indian families.

During the period in which Indians were barred from entering, legal immigration virtually stopped, but many Punjabis continued to come to the United States. Between 1917 and 1930, about 3,000 Asian Indians entered the country illegally by traveling first to Mexico and then sneaking across the border. However, this type of undocumented immigration stopped when the Great Depression of the 1930s, caused by a massive stock market crash in October 1929, turned the United States into an undesirable destination for emigrants around the world.

The restrictions on Asian Indian immigration lasted for almost three decades. After World War II, the U.S. government lifted racist bans on immigration and set small quotas (numerical limits) for the number of Asian Indians and other nationalities that could enter the country each year. With these changes, Asian Indian Americans could finally send for their families, who were exempt from yearly quotas and no longer barred. Most of the Asian Indian immigrants arriving in the United States between 1947 and 1965 were related to the Sikhs who had settled in California decades earlier.

However, immigrants from other parts of India also arrived after 1947. In that year, India gained its independence from Great Britain. The new Indian government retained many of the institutions the British had developed, including an excellent educational

A woman waits for food from a distribution center in rural India in 1967. Severe famine in the 1960s forced many Asian Indians to emigrate.

system. The system produced highly skilled professionals who looked to the United States as one place to continue their training. Though most of the Asian Indian immigrants who arrived between 1947 and 1965 were Punjabis who obtained visas though their families, at least 1,500 other immigrants came as students and professionals hoping to round out an exceptional education.

Economic Distress

In the 1960s, the United States again changed its immigration policy, this time making all quotas equal at 20,000 people per country each year. Suddenly the restrictions that had kept Asian Indians from going to the United States were lifted.

The timing of this new immigration freedom coincided with some devastating conditions in India. At first, India's new independent government under Prime Minister Jawaharlal Nehru had been very successful, implementing two Five-Year Plans (1950–1955 and 1956–1961) that helped industrialize the nation. But the second plan was more ambitious than the first and pushed the people to produce more than they could. By 1966, there was an unprecedented food shortage in India, with many states approaching famine conditions. In addition, the country was plagued by inflation, and the industrial growth and production characteristic of the 1950s slowed considerably in the mid–1960s. The rupee, the currency of India, was devalued in 1966, so that the money could no longer buy as much as before.

In 1967, Indira Gandhi, the daughter of the late prime minister Nehru, gained enough support to become prime minister herself. Throughout the late 1960s and the 1970s, she implemented radical measures to help the economy, such as nationalizing, or putting under government control, all the banks in India. Early on, the measures were effective in increasing food production and alleviating some of the country's economic distress. But soon Gandhi met with opposition and was forced to sweep drastic government controls through Parliament in order to maintain her power. By the mid-1970s, Gandhi declared a state of emergency, censoring the press and outlawing strikes to quell dissent, measures that were approved by Parliament. At the same time, she initiated a program of economic reform to curb inflation, stimulate production, and rein in unemployment.

Gandhi's program improved the economy somewhat, but the manner in which it controlled the people was stifling. One of her reforms was to stem the bursting population of India by activating a birth control program that approached forced sterilization of men. The government controls included incentives for the workers who carried them out, leading to widespread corruption, bribery and inefficiency.

Though the entire population of India was affected by these conditions, only the educated were likely to emigrate to escape the economic and social situation. Others did not have the resources to leave, nor did they have the skills that would be welcome in other countries. Educated professionals were trained by nationally funded universities for careers that the government could no longer offer them. In 1970, there were 20,000 physicians out of work and in 1974, 100,000 engineers were jobless. The salaries of those professionals who were employed did not reflect the amount of education and training they had received.

Gandhi's political party, the Indian National Congress, was defeated in a 1977 election, and she resigned as prime minister. Although accusations about corruption surfaced in the next year, her popularity was not diminished and she was returned to office in 1980.

Efforts in the 1980s and 1990s by Gandhi's successors to return some control of industry to private owners stimulated growth at first. But the Indian government remained in massive debt to other countries, and inflation reached 17 percent in 1990. The government alleviated some of the economic distress in 1991 by completely removing government control of industry and luring private corporations to take over business in India. But the enormous failure in past decades of government-owned industry has proved an insurmountable obstacle. Only the wealthiest were getting richer. The poor were struggling for their share, and a class war was waging. India became a corrupt and violent society.

Religious Conflict

The violence in India is not solely motivated by economic factors. Not only are the formerly government-controlled factories burdened with outdated technology borrowed from the Soviet Union in the 1970s, leaving many bankrupt and useless, but an explosive religious situation throughout the country drives away many potential investors.

When Britain organized India as a colony, it threw together states once divided by religion and language. The current borders of India reflect a haphazard union of many dissimilar societies.

continued on page 19

15

Asha Singh
One People

Asha Singh is 55 years old and lives in Los Angeles. She and her husband arrived 25 years ago from the Punjab region of India.

I have raised a family of four sons and two daughters. We have given them a good life, relatively free of religious strife and economic struggle. We have educated them and seen them prosper. I am 55 years old and content that I have done my job. I have grandchildren now. I worry more for them than I did my own children. My own children were more protected in the Sikh community. My grandchildren participate more in the American way of life.

My husband is respected in our community and at work. He is the president of a computer consulting firm. It is based in India, but has branches in the United States. We came to this country so that he could work and be rewarded. We came to this country to worship in peace. All in all these things have happened. We experienced some resurgence of hatred for our religion after the assassination of Indira Gandhi by her Sikh bodyguards. Even here in Los Angeles, people were treating us cruelly—especially white Americans. It seems strange that we would be punished for a crime that happened in India, but people are strange. It is hard to explain religious persecution. I can say that I have experienced prejudice here, but not persecution.

We live in a very close-knit community of fellow Sikhs. Although my husband works with many different people, I myself only associate with those in my community. This is not because I have animosity toward others, but because I do not come in contact for the most part with anyone else. It is different for my children, both

my sons and my daughters. I feel my daughters have become more independent in America than if they had stayed in India. My husband does not see this as a particularly good quality. I never disagree with him, but silently I think it is a fine thing. I am very proud of all my children's accomplishments.

What can I say about my life that any good mother wouldn't say? I have prepared good food and cleaned and provided a home that is pleasant to the eye and warm to be in. My husband and I share a deep dedication to our family and our religion. They are one and the same to us.

Perhaps I do feel a bit of an outcast at times. I see the looks when we shop. People still find it strange to see a man in a business suit and a turban. Yet we have not suffered some of the more outward attacks that we read about others suffering. If I feel anything, it is mostly misunderstood. How does one explain oneself to people with so many strange preconceptions?

I believe things are changing. My children tell me this and I have seen it myself only recently. I was in a shopping mall, resting on a bench. A young woman sat next to me and we began to talk. She actually asked if I was Sikh and didn't just assume I was Hindu. When I said yes, she smiled and pointed to a button on her jacket. She was a blond girl, in her twenties maybe. The button she had on was this one. See? (She pointed to her button.) I wear it on my sari now. It is just a picture of the earth taken from space and on the top it says "One God," and on the bottom, "One People." This girl said she got it from Sikhs in Chicago at the World Conference of Religions. She said it was a very popular button there. I was surprised when she gave it to me and very touched.

Doesn't that give you hope? A conference where all the world's religions came together not to convert or fight each other, but to just talk and understand. I have been much happier about the state of the world since meeting that young woman. I think of her often. I am particularly proud that the Sikhs made this button.

I have to say that I dream of India often. Some mornings I wake up and ache to be there. Then I begin to think of the reality of that dream and it fades. I know now that my husband and I will live here until we die. Our children are Americans. And if we truly are "One People," then perhaps it doesn't matter where I live.

Most Indians are Hindus, and Hindus control the government. But there exist substantial minorities of Muslims (11%) and Sikhs (2%) in India, who both contend that the Hindu government tries to suppress their religions. Currently, at least three of the country's border states are under virtual martial law (in which the military replaces civilian government and law enforcement) because of unrest and separatist movements led by religious minorities. In addition, the strict caste system of the Hindus, which divides all people into separate classes that are forbidden to mix, has led to mistreatment of the lower castes and, often, blatant racism.

Hindus believe that all people are born into a caste determined by one's karma (fate). Hindus also believe in reincarnation. The acts one committed during a past lifetime determine present karma. And the acts committed in a present lifetime determine whether an individual will move from lower, polluted castes to a higher, pure caste until nirvana (eternal afterlife) is achieved.

There are more than 3,000 caste designations, but they can all be categorized into four major castes, called varnas, meaning "color." Lighter-skinned people tend to be in the higher castes. The highest caste are Brahmins, the learned caste. Below that are Kshatriyas, the warrior caste, and Vaisyas, who are traders and merchants. The lowest caste are the Sudras, who are destined to be laborers and servants. But below the Sudras are the outcastes, known as Harijans. They are considered impure and "untouchable" and are delegated the most despised jobs, like cleaning sewers. Up to three fourths of India's population are Sudras or Harijans. Most Hindu Asian Indian Americans are from the Brahmin and Kshatriya castes.

Currently, it is illegal in India to discriminate based on caste,

An outcaste family in Patna, India. Though the Indian government has outlawed the caste system, many Hindus still shun those considered "untouchable."

and some liberal politicians have campaigned on the platform of affirmative action for the lower castes. But caste still plays a major role in social relationships, especially in rural areas. Intermarriage with a Harijan could lead to death for both people, usually by mob beating or lynching. Outcastes are commonly killed in India for not obeying the rules of this five-century-old system. Outcaste children in rural villages are kept from schools, while upper caste children are educated. Different castes get their water from different wells, evoking images of a segregated South in the United States fifty years ago.

Virtually the only escape for Hindus from the prejudice, unfairness, and racism of the caste system is religious conversion to Islam, Sikhism, or Christianity. Some middle-class Indians have attempted to move up through the castes by becoming professionals and imitating the devout religiousness of the upper castes. It is these middle-class professionals who are likely to emigrate because they want to live where caste does not affect their lives.

For non-Hindu minorities, however, political control is the biggest concern. Since the first days of independence, after Britain's Indian colony was divided into separate states of India and Pakistan and thousands of Indian Muslims migrated to Pakistan, religious minorities have been fighting for greater self-rule. Since 1990, Muslim separatists have pushed for independence of Kashmir, a mostly Islamic state in the north of India. Violence is common in Uttar Pradesh and Gujarat between Muslims and Sikhs trying to control the states. And secessionist wars are continually being fought in Punjab, a mostly Sikh state. Many of these wars are closely tied to economic divisions as well.

Since two Sikh members of Indira Gandhi's personal bodyguard assassinated her in October 1984, conflict between the Indian government and the Sikhs has escalated. The assassination occurred after government officers led a massacre of 1,000 people at the Golden Temple, the holiest Sikh shrine. Gandhi's son, Rajiv, was immediately sworn in as prime minister and was confirmed by elections within six weeks. Attempts by Rajiv Gandhi to unite the people of India only met with Sikh extremism, and Sikh terrorism intensified throughout the 1980s. The violence reached its peak in 1991, when 5,000 died in battles between Sikh militants and police and army units. The situation was worsened when Rajiv Gandhi was assassinated in 1991 by those protesting India's involvement in the affairs of its neighbor, Sri Lanka.

The Muslim minority has found cause to protest their treatment by the Hindus as well. A highly publicized attack in 1992 on a sixteenth-century Muslim mosque was carried out by Hindus who claimed that the mosque was built on the birth site of Ram, a Hindu god. Dozens of men stormed the mosque with sledgehammers, destroying the structure with the tacit approval of Hindu leaders. Subsequent protests by Muslims in cities around India led to violence and more attacks on them by Hindu mobs. Since that incident, tensions between Hindus and Muslims have intensified.

The government has responded to economic and religious uprisings with what human rights groups say includes torture, unlawful detention, and murder. Amnesty International reports that "disappearances" are common, referring to the practice by some governments of kidnapping dissidents who are then never seen again. Government officials, according to Amnesty, "have subverted legal proceedings initiated to clarify 'disappearances.'" As a result, violence in some states like Punjab has diminished,

On December 6, 1992, Hindu militants stormed a Muslim mosque they believed was built on a sacred Hindu site. Religious violence has increased throughout India, causing many non-Hindus to leave the country.

but so has personal freedom. Residents say peace has been restored by local police terror. Sikhs and Hindus alike provide reports of police-led attacks, rapes, and murders.

Muslim and Sikh emigrants leave India in the hopes of escaping from those areas where the violence doesn't appear to be diminishing. They seek political asylum, a claim reserved for those who fear for their lives at the hands of their governments. Many Muslims and Sikhs fear the repercussions of belonging to a religious minority in a Hindu-run state. Most of these political emigrants are from the educated middle class, and possess technical skills that will help establish them in a new country.

Living Conditions

For many, the drive to leave India comes not from the violence but from the unpleasant living conditions and the sheer lack of privacy. India is the second most populous country in the world, and the leader in population density. In 1992 an average of 695 lived in each square mile of India. Compare that with the United States, where an average of 71 people inhabited each square mile. And the population of India grows by more than 17 million people each year. At last count, the country held more than 880 million people. By the year 2000, India will become the most populous country in the world and only the second country (after the People's Republic of China) with over a billion people.

These conditions create noisy, crowded cities. In addition, natural resources are drying up. Illegal deforestation to provide for fuel and to make room for crop planting is creating an environmen-

tal disaster, and Indians are forced to go farther and farther for their fuel and water. The water supply is badly polluted by sewage and toxic dumping. Even some of Hinduism's sacred rivers, such as the Ganges and the Jamuna, are without biological life and are chemically hazardous to humans. And the air quality in India's cities has been rated among the worst in the world; at the same time, average life expectancy is among the lowest.

Poverty is rampant. Almost half the residents of Bombay, the world's seventh largest city, are squatters, people who live illegally in any spaces they can find. Child labor is common. One third of children are born with irreversible malnutrition. And hand in hand with poverty is illiteracy. India's literacy rate barely exceeds 50 percent (in the United States, it's 97 percent); in remote rural areas, the literacy rate dips to 2 percent.

Attempts by the government to solve these problems have

A public bus in India with a capacity limit of 56 carries more than 150 passengers at once on an average day.

bogged down the country in red tape. Government officials are often rewarded for meeting quotas rather than producing change. Thus, a woman in a remote rural area who is well past the age of childbearing may be given a contraceptive by a doctor hoping to meet unreasonable quotas for population control. Roads may deliberately be built poorly so that they must be rebuilt each year, and be counted on the next year's construction lists. A pump may be installed in a village well so that the village will be listed as having water, but if the pump breaks down, no one fixes it.

Deplorable conditions exist in both the villages, home to 70 percent of India's population, and the cities, among the most crowded in the world. There are few pristine areas of India left, and most Asian Indians looking to escape inferior living conditions soon realize they must leave the country to do so.

= 2 =

Why the United States?

The Early Sojourners

Though the Sikhs constitute only 2 percent of the population in India, up to 90 percent of the Asian Indians that settled on the West Coast beginning in 1907 were Sikhs from Punjab.

Having left that state to escape land shortages and famine conditions, the Sikh farmers sought a place where they could earn money and support their families. Some joined the British army, traveling throughout Asia and fighting in 1900 in the Boxer Rebellion in China. And since the Sikhs had come from a colony of the British Crown, it was natural that some would go to Australia or other British lands.

Many went to Canada, then still a British holding, where the newly constructed railroad was creating a boom town in Vancouver, British Columbia. Vancouver's location, in Puget Sound just above Washington State, made it an ideal port town for goods coming in from Asia.

But in the early 1900s, racial hostility in Canada drove the Asian Indians out of the country. Some returned to India, but many migrated south to northern Washington, where there were jobs available in the logging industry. Once there, they branched out to other parts of the state and south to Oregon and California.

The United States was an appealing location to these former

farmers for many reasons. Most could speak some English or at least could ally with Indians who had once served in the army of the British Empire and who could then act as translators for a large group. Wages in the United States were very high compared with those in India—two dollars a day versus ten cents—and hard workers could hope to save enough money within a few years to buy or lease some land of their own.

The opportunity to buy or lease land was one of the greatest draws for the Punjabis. In 1907 the West had been only recently settled, and much of it was ripe for farming. California was particularly attractive to Punjabis because many of the same crops they had farmed in India were also grown in the Sacramento or Yuba valleys. Their skills and knowledge made them an asset to the local landowners.

The Ban Is Lifted

For the years between the Great Depression and the end of World War II, immigration from India was almost completely halted. But after the war, Congress passed a law granting Indians and other Asians the right to immigrate again and to become citizens of the United States. Though immigration was limited by quotas of only 100 people per year from India, the quotas did not apply to relatives of Asian Indian citizens.

As a result, between 1947 and 1965 the Asian Indian communities in California were revived by a surge of immigration. Husbands sent for the wives and family members they had not seen for decades, and bachelors journeyed to India to marry and return with their new brides. Older men sponsored their younger relatives as immigrants. What was close to becoming a lost ethnic community of Asian Indians received new life.

Many of the new immigrants to California were farmers, like their Punjabi predecessors. But there were also many educated Asian Indians. With its high rate of engineering graduates, Punjab contributed many Sikhs lured by the growing defense and computer industries in the 1950s and 1960s.

It wasn't until the 1960s, however, that Asian Indians began immigrating in the overwhelming numbers that continue today. With powerful revisions in its immigration law, the United States threw open the door, previously closed to most Asian immigration, to highly educated groups like Asian Indians.

The Surge Begins

In 1965, President Lyndon Johnson signed the Immigration and Nationality Act, the product of planning by the administrations of Johnson and his predecessor, John F. Kennedy. After years of quotas that discriminated against Asians and other non-Europeans, the government took steps to eliminate racism in its immigration policy. It set the annual limit on immigrants from each country at 20,000, regardless of continent, race, or religion. And in the interest of keeping families united, the immediate relatives of U.S. citizens and permanent residents were designated exempt from these quotas.

For Asian Indians, the new quotas resulted in an immediate increase in immigration. The United States represented a haven from some of the problems plaguing India. But more than that, the United States offered employment and economic opportunities not available in India.

Three young Indian women arrive by ship to attend college in the United States on scholarships granted by the State Department and administered by the Institute of International Education.

The structure of the new immigration law created preference categories for different education, training, and skill levels. Thus, the foreigners most welcome by the United States were highly educated professionals, artists, and businesspeople. Physicians, engineers, scientists, professors, teachers, and businesspeople poured into the United States through qualifications obtained in India.

The Asian Indians who came to the United States differed from the ones who emigrated elsewhere. Though Indians went to other English-speaking countries–such as Great Britain, Canada, and Australia–most of the professionals opted to come to the United States. Two types of professionals in particular were most common among Asian Indian immigrants in the 1970s and 1980s: physicians, because there was an acute shortage in the United States in those decades, and computer science engineers, because they were vital to a booming industry.

In the late 1960s and early 1970s, the United States needed more doctors and nurses, and the government began to attract foreign medical personnel to fill in the gaps. Many of the first Indian immigrants were doctors who received their undergraduate medical training in India and came to the United States to complete their residencies. By 1976, India was the source of most of this country's foreign physicians.

In India, universities, and especially medical schools, are modeled on European and American schools. Courses are often taught in English. But in India, the emphasis is on specialization, resulting in many specialists who then compete for the few positions around the country.

The United States is noted for its superior medical education and research opportunities, making it a magnet for foreign doctors seeking the best training. In particular, India contributes many

≡ *31* ≡   *continued on page 35*

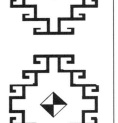

Gita Chandar
Big American Dreams

Gita Chandar is 20 years old. She is an art major at Middle Tennessee State University in Murfreesboro.

I was born in Oak Ridge, Tennessee, where the nuclear research laboratory is located. My father received his Ph.D. in physics at Massachusetts Institute of Technology. He met my mother in Boston. She's a laboratory technician. Anyway, what I was trying to get at is, he ended up in Tennessee because the job at Oak Ridge was the only one he could get in America, and he wanted to stay. He worked there for almost ten years, but he never thought he was getting anywhere. Don't ask me to explain that because I don't really understand science or management decisions all that much. I just know that he ended up teaching at Vanderbilt University in Nashville, and I'm glad he did. So is my mother. She works there, too. She's the head of a lab now.

I'm going to be a filmmaker. I was just accepted to the graduate film program at the University of Southern California. I say that calmly but I am very amazed. I study painting and film at MTSU. I haven't really had that much experience in film in this country, but my uncle is a prominent director in India. I have worked for him on several films. I even took a semester leave once to work on a film in Bombay. I'm very lucky.

To tell the truth, I mostly like American films. I respect a director like Satyajit Ray and was very happy to see him honored at the Academy Awards. But I guess I prefer films that are, well, more American! Did you see the movie *Mississippi Masala*? Well, that was a great American film made by an Indian woman. I liked it for lots of reasons, but one thing I really liked was that she talked about race in America. I also liked seeing an Indian woman star in a movie. It made me more determined than ever to be a filmmaker. You don't see people like me very often in the movies, and I am going to change that. Everyone needs to see themselves.

Since I was born here, I am an American, but as you can see I still feel very Indian, too. Even if I didn't know a lot of Indian friends of my family and visit India and eat Indian food often, I would still feel Indian because people treat me as if I am. It is hard to explain. It is not so much people treating me poorly. It is just a way of people acting as if you are foreign because of the way you look. I have quite a few friends here at school, both black and white, and I think it took them a while to realize that I am not so different than they are.

My family is pretty rare, I think, for Indian immigrants. My mother does not dress traditionally at work. She wears the same lab coat and pants as everyone else. She sometimes wears a sari to festive occasions within the Indian community here, but that is about it. She never worries about how I dress. Nor does my dad. They pretty much let my younger brother and sister participate in the same social life as the rest of the kids. They go to University School like I did. It is a pretty cool place. It is a private school and lots of professors' kids go there. What that means is that quite a few of the kids have parents from other countries. It just makes you feel more comfortable.

Although my family is Hindu, it is more as if we have no religion. We only go to a temple maybe once a year. Both of my parents meditate on the weekend, but they have never required that we children do so. Maybe that was wise. I have recently begun to meditate on my own and set up a small shrine in my room. Sometimes I think that you can never turn your back on India.

My mother has a book on Indian miniature painting. I used to look at it all the time when I was a child. The paintings tell so many stories of Indian history and folktales and Hindu gods. I thought I closed the book when I went to study painting at MTSU, but I didn't. I look at my own paintings and I see the vivid colors and details from that book. I guess I even want to make films like that in a way, rich in color and detail.

I don't know how to say exactly who I am. The closest I can come would be to say that I am an Asian Indian woman with big American dreams.

specialists in the fields of anesthesiology, radiology, and pathology, though doctors from all disciplines immigrate here. One in 4 Asian Indian professionals in the United States is a physician and 1 in 20 physicians in the United States is Asian Indian.

In the 1970s and 1980s, work in the American computer industry was expanding rapidly. California's Silicon Valley sprouted new hardware and software companies, and Asian Indians flocked to participate in the development of new technology.

Most of the engineers were Sikhs from Punjab and other northern states of India. They were drawn to the recently rejuvenated communities of Sikhs that had existed in California since the turn of the century. Rather than to continue to struggle with a lack of infrastructure (roads, telecommunications, etc.) in India, the engineers decided to bring their considerable talents to the United States. Many work for Indian computer companies that have the engineering talent but not the resources to manufacture computer systems and software. These companies work with American manufacturers and link the technology in India (the third largest source of software engineers after the United States and France) with American manufacturers.

Refugees from Africa

During the 1970s, some Asian Indians arrived not from India but from their adopted home, Uganda. When parts of east Africa were under British rule, Asian Indians had been recruited to work there as representatives of the British crown. In the 1960s, Asian Indians constituted a large minority in some of these countries, particularly Uganda.

This hastily-shot photo shows the urgency with which Asian Indians were trying to escape Uganda in 1972 after Idi Amin announced all Indians must leave within 90 days. Many refugees eventually settled in the United States.

By the late 1960s, however, most African nations had gained or were about to gain their independence. In Uganda, a dictator by the name of Idi Amin took power and soon began a campaign against the Asian Indian minority. Most of the Indians were wealthy business owners, and Amin believed they were partly responsible for the poverty among the African natives. Amin instituted a program of discrimination against the Asian Indians, confiscating their businesses and, in 1972, expelling tens of thousands of them from the country. Some returned to India or emigrated to Britain, but many fled to the United States seeking political asylum.

Generally, those who came to the United States entered the same business: they became motel owners. In the early 1970s, interest rates were extremely low, especially compared with interest rates in India. Motels were inexpensive businesses, and 95 percent of the purchase price could be paid for with loans. Asian Indians took advantage of the low interest rates to take out mortgages and buy motels. With the purchases, they bought not only prosperous businesses, but instant homes and places to employ large extended families.

Today, Asian Indians dominate the motel industry in some areas of the United States. Most of the owners were originally from the state of Gujarat, so word of their success quickly spread among friends and acquaintances. The majority of Indian-owned motels are in California, Georgia, Oklahoma, Texas, and Mississippi.

A New Wave of Families

When immigrants come to this country, they inevitably create a new surge of immigration by sponsoring their relatives. United States immigration law favors the reunification of families, and any permanent resident can sponsor a family member to enter the United States.

Throughout its history, immigration to the United States has begotten more immigration, producing a phenomenon known as chain migration. One immigrant may be responsible for the subsequent immigration of dozens from his or her homeland, as relatives turn around and sponsor spouses and more relatives.

In recent years fewer Asian Indian immigrants are arriving through their professional qualifications while more are immigrating with family sponsorships. Often, today's immigrants use this avenue because they don't qualify under strict U.S. preferences. They are not as well educated or as skilled as their predecessors. For less educated emigrants, the destination choices are limited. Although they still reach out to Britain, strict immigration laws there and a poor economy have kept them away in recent years. Some choose to work in the Middle East in the oil industry, but differences in lifestyle and language can be deterrents. More often, emigrants will choose to come to the United States. The language, culture, and lifestyles of Americans are familiar to Indians through imported movies and television.

But economics may be the primary attraction for Asian Indian workers, both professional and nonprofessional. Salaries in India are low, barely one tenth of U.S. salaries for technically qualified workers. Many Asian Indian Americans begin their immigration to the United States as students and refuse to return to India because their salary expectations have risen to U.S. standards.

What Is Their Journey Like?

Leaving Punjabi Lands Behind

For many of the first Asian Indian immigrants to North America, the journey started not with a passenger ticket purchased at great expense but with military orders issued by a commanding officer. Some of the emigrants in the early 20th century first left India by joining the British Army, where they served in Singapore, Hong Kong, and Australia. These were the younger sons of the Sikh farmers, forced to find work to keep their families' lands intact.

But as soldiers, Indians found that the British had little respect for them. Some white officers looked down on the Indian soldiers, and even refused to recognize fellow officers who were Indians. Many Indians, frustrated and disillusioned, resigned from the army and looked to Canada for their new home. There they joined the Asian Indians who had preceded them to North America. Many actually made the trip in groups, pooling their resources.

The trip across the Pacific to Vancouver cost a considerable sum—about 300 rupees. Veterans were most likely to have the cash on hand, but civilians were forced to sell family jewels or mortgage their share of the family property. Considering that property was the item they were trying to save by going abroad, such mortgages were extremely risky. But because they expected to return in a

Sikhs first came to farm land along the West Coast, starting a farming tradition that continues today. These 1940s Sikh farmers are learning how to use new equipment.

short time and reclaim their land, the debt seemed worth the risk.

The actual voyage began by train, on a rail system the British had built to transport India's natural resources more easily. The train took the Indians, who were usually from the villages close to the railroad, to Delhi where they boarded another train to Calcutta. From Calcutta they boarded a boat to Hong Kong, where they caught a steamship to Vancouver. Some even stopped in Fiji or Australia on the way.

This was not a quick journey. The trains were slow and the boats out of Hong Kong were few and far between. Along the way, Sikh immigrants could count on the hospitality of Sikh temples in

Delhi, Calcutta, and even Hong Kong (established by soldiers stationed there). But once into the Pacific crossing, they had to endure weeks of overcrowding, bad weather, and food more familiar to Chinese than Indians.

Vancouver was a boom town, recently connected to the rest of Canada by the railroad. There, Punjabis became more westernized, changing their dress and learning English. British Columbia promised much work in lumbering, especially because mill owners knew they could pay the Asian Indians less.

Within a few years, word had spread of the steady work available just a little farther south. Asian Indians found employment in the lumber mills of northern Washington State, especially in the town of Bellingham. From Bellingham, the Sikhs moved south to California, as opportunities in railroad work and farming opened up. They settled in the Sacramento, Imperial, and Yuba valleys, where pockets of Asian Indian communities still exist.

More and more Asian Indians began to make their way to the West Coast of the United States instead of making the journey to Canada first. Asian Indian immigrants, having heard in letters of the two dollars a day they could earn in the United States, boarded steamships in Hong Kong that would take them directly to San Francisco, Portland, or Seattle.

Across the Mexican Border and Around the Law

When the U.S. government passed a 1917 law prohibiting immigration from certain Asian countries, Asian Indians' hopes of earning their fortunes in the United States were shattered. But

continued on page 45

Sharma Dutt
Blossoms and Land

Sharma Dutt is 47 years old and lives just outside of Marysville, California, where there is a large community of Asian Indians from the Punjab region of India. She came to this country in 1950 when she was three years old. She owns India Palace, a store that sells foods and items from India.

Although I was raised in California and am an American citizen, I still feel mostly Punjabi. My father's great-uncle had been in this country since 1910, so there was an established community here of people from the Punjab. I grew up within an Indian community. Yet I am proud that I come from a family that has been in America for so long. Somehow this makes me feel more like I belong here.

Well, this sounds like a lot of contradiction, doesn't it? I guess it is just my way to say that I like being an Asian Indian American. My culture is very important to me, but I am glad to be here in northern California. My father owns almond orchards. It was good to be a child surrounded by blossoms and land. I always knew I would somehow stay here with my family.

After high school, I went first to a local junior college. I had in my mind to be a teacher. But after taking all the basic requirements, I discovered I liked business. This was a good surprise. I then went to Sacramento State to get a business and accounting degree. I was proud, and thought maybe I could work for a big company and become a vice president or something! After graduating I did take an accounting job in Sacramento for a short time—very short. That fall I went home and met my future husband. He had arrived from India that summer. He had an engineering degree and was only going to stay for a while in Marysville and visit relatives

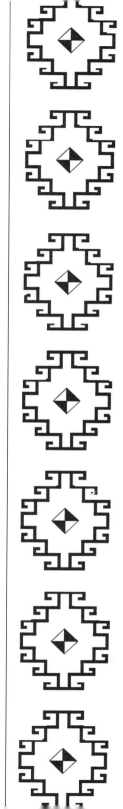

before leaving for the Bay Area. Needless to say, things didn't happen that way.

We married and he went into farming with my father and brother. He loves it to this day. He and my brother get along so well that my father says it's as if they are brothers. The farm is quite large and prosperous now. My husband does very well, but in the beginning we struggled a bit and I had to work. I was a clerk in an office equipment store and did not like it very much. I saved my money and opened a small store not so different from the other Indian stores in the area. Well, it was a little different because I decorated the windows with things both Indian (silk scarves, incense) and American (books, picture frames). They were very beautiful. I attracted not only the Punjabi community but also people from other communities as well. I like meeting new people. I don't have to work now, but I do because I enjoy it so much.

India Palace is much bigger than it used to be. I now carry videos of films from India. Strange as it sounds, these films are all I have ever seen of India. I also have a well-known collection of recipes for Indian foods that I give out for free to people who buy the spices and canned items I carry. I like being a store owner. No one interferes with how I handle my business. I don't think I would be allowed such independence as a woman if I were still in India. I make a moderate amount of money. This especially helped when the children were in college.

They have both graduated already. They are a more modern generation. My oldest son followed his mother's path and went into business. He has an MBA and works for a multinational corporation in San Francisco. My youngest went to the University of California at Davis and studied agricultural engineering. He works on designing new, more efficient ways to harvest crops. He is a researcher on staff at Davis.

I am surprised that neither one wants to farm with their father. My husband still thinks that the youngest will eventually come back and take his place. Maybe he is

right. Both our sons are American in that way: they want to do it on their own first.

As you can probably tell, I'm glad to be here. Not that there haven't been problems, maybe more now than when I was young. So many people have come to this area from the Punjab over the years that instead of being a curiosity to the town, we are now perceived as a threat. I read letters to the editor in the local paper that are very hostile to our presence. This is hard to understand because my community works very hard and is respectful of everyone. The letters sometimes say, Why don't we dress like Americans? As you can see, I still wear a sari although it is modified by American pants underneath. Our men wear turbans. This especially seems to bother people. We try to explain that this is a religious act, not a fashion statement. As Sikhs, our men are required to cover their heads in this manner. It is a daily devotion, like the Catholics who go to mass every morning.

We have relatives and friends who live in smaller towns near here. Many of them work irrigating the rice for the big landowners. Some own small parcels of rice land themselves. They say that sometimes people call them "ragheads" because of their turbans. This is so painful for me to hear. I know that this country was founded on religious tolerance, so I can't understand this kind of attack.

Not to complain too much, though. There are problems everywhere. My husband and I are very happy to be here. Why shouldn't we be? After all, this is our home.

some determined emigrants decided to risk illegal immigration to make their way to the land of opportunity.

Until 1929, the Mexican-U.S. border was open—Mexicans needed to pay only five dollars to cross. There were no restrictions on Mexican immigration, even at a time when European immigrants were screened carefully at Ellis Island before being permitted to enter New York. Moreover, the U.S. border with Mexico is almost 2,000 miles long, and much of it is marked by shallow riverbeds and invisible lines in the desert. Crossing the border did not always mean driving on an established road and stopping for a border guard. The Border Patrol that polices the 2,000 miles today did not exist in the 1920s.

Between 1920 and 1930, as many as 3,000 Asian Indians immigrated to the United States through Mexico. After taking a steamship from Hong Kong to ports like Acapulco, they would travel along Baja to the California border and sneak across at points not patrolled by border guards. Others would just walk or drive across the border, disguising themselves as Mexicans and paying the five dollar fee. Few border guards knew enough about the difference between a Mexican and an Asian Indian to know that one was not allowed in the country.

Immigration After 1965

The Asian Indians that immigrate to the United States today do not have the same worries as their predecessors. In most cases, they are educated enough to speak English comfortably. They rarely have to risk the kind of debt incurred by turn-of-the-century immigrants to pay for passage, because they come from the middle and upper-middle classes. However, they do have one obstacle that the Punjabis didn't have in 1907: the wait for visa approval.

A visa is a document the government of a country grants to a noncitizen, allowing that person to travel, work, or live in the country. The United States issues immigrant visas and nonimmigrant visas, depending on whether a person wants to stay permanently or just visit. Asian Indians who want to move here need immigrant visas.

Under the changes in immigration laws implemented in the 1960s, the immigrants who had the greatest chance of obtaining an immigrant visa were those who had special skills needed in the United States. That category included, of course, physicians, because the country was experiencing a shortage, and engineers, as the United States was competing with the Soviet Union and Japan in the development of new technology. Other preferences included persons with advanced degrees, established artists and performers, scientists, and others with "extraordinary" and "exceptional" abilities. Unskilled workers could immigrate as well, but they were often forced to wait many years before visas became available to them. Sometimes the wait was as long as ten years.

Under the most recent changes to U.S. immigration law, passed in 1990, the category for unskilled workers was completely eliminated (though those already waiting for visas would still be granted them). In addition, family-preference visas were assigned a quota for the first time. Immigrants trying to join their families are no longer allowed unlimited entry. Overall, the annual quota per country increased to more than 25,000, though each country's quota depends on a complicated formula. Basically the new quotas slightly favor nationalities whose immigration has dropped off, particularly

northern Europeans, and slightly handicap nationalities that have had increasing immigration in the last decades, such as Asians.

Many of the Asian Indian immigrants here today came originally as students and decided to stay once they realized that job opportunities in India were not as good as those in the United States. At first, anyone who wanted to stay could merely follow the visa application process like other immigrants. But changes in immigration laws in the 1970s and 1980s required that foreign students in certain professions go back to their home countries and work for two years before coming to work in the United States.

These laws were enacted partly to alleviate what is called the "brain drain," the massive migration of educated professionals from Third World countries to the United States and other devel-

Changes in immigration laws since 1965 help families stay together when coming to the United States.

oped countries. The framers of the laws hoped that those who went back to their native countries would stay. But the laws also helped American citizens apply for jobs without the added competition of new immigrants. Some of the countries that the law was intended to help have been known to waive the two-year requirement, believing that the money sent back by a worker in America will be more helpful to the economy than the two years of work. But the U.S. State Department, in the interest of helping American workers, will not always recognize the waiver.

Undocumented Immigrants

Many Asian Indians begin their journeys to the United States with non-immigrant visas. These are given either for travel or for work or study. Recently, more and more Asian Indians have been coming to the United States on tourist visas—which allow travel only for one year—and staying after their visas run out. Some students and temporary workers have also ignored visa limitations. Overstaying a visa is illegal, and those who get caught in the United States after their visas expire can be deported (sent back to their native country). But a majority of violators don't get caught.

Other Asian Indians who don't want to wait for immigrant visas try sneaking into the country, usually through the same route Indians took in the 1920s. Only this time, the trip through Mexico and across the border is not as easy or as inexpensive. Asian Indians hoping to sneak into the United States must first travel to Europe and then to Mexico City on a tourist visa. There they hire a coyote, a smuggler of people. Coyotes are paid between

$2,000 and $3,000 to hide immigrants in a car trunk while cross-ing into the United States or to take the immigrants to the shal-lowest points of the Rio Grande, where they try to wade across into U.S. land without being caught by the Border Patrol.

An immigrant who overstays a visa or enters the country without one becomes an undocumented immigrant, also known as an illegal immigrant. Without the proper documents, such as a per-manent resident card or a Social Security card, immigrants can't get a job unless they lie, use a fake name, or otherwise break the law. They live every day in fear of being caught and deported.

Some Asian Indians use a legal loophole to remain in the country without an immigrant visa. According to U.S. laws, if a person arriving in the United States asks for political asylum, he or she is automatically granted a work permit, and a date is set for an asylum hearing. Political asylum is granted to immigrants who fear that their lives or freedom would be in danger if they returned to their country. Many Asian Indian Sikhs have legitimate claims for political asylum because of the violent situation in Punjab. But others use the claim merely as a ruse to get into the country. They usually come through John F. Kennedy International Airport in New York because it has no facility for detaining asylum seekers—whereas the airport in Los Angeles does have such a facility. The immigrant at JFK is automatically released. The U.S. government is working to change asylum laws so that asylum seekers must pay a fee for their claim and wait for work permits.

Most Asian Indian Americans immigrate to the United States legally. But for those who entered illegally before 1986, a special law that year granted them amnesty, a chance to become legal residents. If they could prove they had lived in this country for five years continuously, they were given permanent resident status, and no legal action was brought against them. The immigration laws passed in 1990 created a separate quota for the families of those immigrants who had received amnesty, making it possible for them to reunite their families without qualifying under the stringent preference categories or the newly limited family preference categories. Hundreds of unskilled Asian Indians took advantage of the amnesty provisions.

This Sikh man lives in New York City. Many Sikh's fled India because they suffered from religious persecution.

The Paperwork

Once an Asian Indian has qualified for rigorous U.S. preference categories, he or she has to face an agonizing mountain of paperwork and a long wait for visas and citizenship. Between the time a foreigner applies for an immigrant visa and the time he or she becomes a citizen, as many as seven years may elapse, and that is if the visa is granted right away.

To get any type of visa, foreigners must go to the U.S. consulate (a branch of the embassy) nearest them with their passports, their birth certificates, and letters from the police saying they are not criminals. They also undergo medical exams to show that they have no contagious diseases. People seeking immigrant visas then fill out a lot of paperwork and wait as their applications are shuttled among several offices in several countries. The visas may not be granted for months or years.

After entering the United States under the authority of an immigrant visa, an Asian Indian immigrant gets a permanent resident card, commonly called a green card. This document allows any noncitizen to live and work in this country without time restrictions, so long as he or she provides a current address to the Immigration and Naturalization Service (INS) once a year.

Green card holders must then wait five years before applying for U.S. citizenship (or three if they are married to a U.S. citizen). After the application for citizenship comes a series of hearings and a citizenship exam that tests the applicant's knowledge of U.S. government and history. The final chapter in the citizenship quest comes when the immigrant is finally sworn in as a citizen. Citizenship entitles a person to a passport, eligibility for certain government jobs, and the right to vote.

Settling in Across the Country

The first Asian Indian Americans lived mostly along the West Coast, but today Asian Indian immigrants can be found in almost every state in the country. In fact, more than one third of Asian

"Little India" in Jackson Heights, Queens, where Asian Indian Americans can find stores specializing in food, clothes, and other goods from their native country.

Indian Americans live in the Northeast, far from their original settlements.

After the 1965 changes to immigration laws, the destinations as well as the numbers of Asian Indians dramatically changed. As more and more American-born professionals moved south and west, away from the old industrial cities of the North and Northeast and toward the new industrial and technological centers like Atlanta and Los Angeles, Asian Indian professionals moved in to take their places. In the inner-city hospitals and the rural Midwest companies, Asian Indians filled the vacuum left by departing professionals and saved many of these institutions from shutting down.

This brought Asian Indians to cities like New York, Chicago, Boston, and Philadelphia. There they took positions as doctors in the city hospitals, which were losing their physicians to the suburbs. Later, as computer companies moved west and south, Asian Indians moved to San Francisco and Oakland, Los Angeles, and Houston.

In areas like 74th Street in the Jackson Heights section of Queens, in New York City, and along Pioneer Boulevard in Artesia, in Los Angeles County, communities nicknamed "Little India" are popping up. They are characterized by Indian clothing stores, restaurants, grocery shops, video stores that specialize in films in one of the 16 languages of India, and even branches of the State Bank of India. The irony of these Little Indias is that, unlike neighborhoods of other ethnic groups, they are merely business or shopping districts and rarely home to many Indians. Local residents have complained about the disappearance of the previous stores and their replacement by the Indian businesses.

Chand Patel
My Third Country

Chand Patel is 51 years old and lives in Abilene, Texas. He owns and operates the Sunset West motel.

I came to Abilene, Texas, in 1972 from Uganda. Oh, I know, that makes people stop and ask a few questions! I was born in India but moved with my father to Uganda. He was a wealthy businessman there for many years, and when I was of age, I became a partner. Three of my children were born in Africa. Then that madman Idi Amin took over Uganda and we had to leave. My parents and brothers returned to India. I wanted a new life. So here I am.

I knew nothing of Texas when we came to the United States. Other Indians we knew from Uganda had come to this country and were buying motels. I thought, now there is a good life.   It was pretty easy to buy a motel since I had come with a good deal of money. We didn't really care where we lived, and when the Sunset West came up for sale, I just bought it. It is a good way of life mostly. We lived in the motel at first and did everything ourselves. My wife and I worked very hard to fix the place up and make it a place where people would want to stop. I know about business, but there was much to learn about motels. Travelers can be a difficult clientele.

We don't live in the motel any longer. We have a house in a new housing development. Very nice. Electric air and heat. Big yard. But we still run the motel. We have added an Indian restaurant to it now, and it is becoming pretty popular. Not only do some of our guests eat here, but we are getting some of the people from town. It took a while for Indian food to catch on in Texas! My wife manages the restaurant now and because more Indian families have moved nearby, we have good cooks to draw on. I've also made a few investments along the way in a pizza parlor and a laundromat. So we're doing pretty good.

The only problem I see happening really is this resentment of some of the other motel owners toward us. It is true that a lot of Indians are buying motels across the country. Is that a problem? Maybe. Sometimes you see signs in windows of motels that say, "American Owned!" That doesn't mean what it says, because we are Americans now. What that means is that an Asian Indian doesn't own that motel. The first time I saw one of those signs, I was very angry. I wanted to go talk to the owner. My wife told me that you don't change the minds of people like that, so just drive on by and keep the peace.

We have some American friends, though we are not very close. It is very Christian here, and we are not Christian. I think most people mingle with people from their church. Our children were the first students of Indian descent to go to school here. It was a little difficult for them at first, but once they showed how well they could do in school, it was easier. Our second oldest son was even a football player! He was very popular. There was a little problem when he began to date one of the cheerleaders. Some of the boys tried to pick fights with him. We finally went to talk to her parents and then things smoothed out. They broke up soon after that, but we are still friends with her parents. You just never know about things.

We are happier now that there are other Indian families nearby. We mostly socialize together. Unlike some of the more recent arrivals, we do not go to India often—actually, only twice since we have been here. It is strange—even though my ties to my culture are strong and I miss my family, I don't really have any connection to the country itself. I wonder about my children and their children. Who will they be? I don't want them to turn out like those young people on television. I say that,

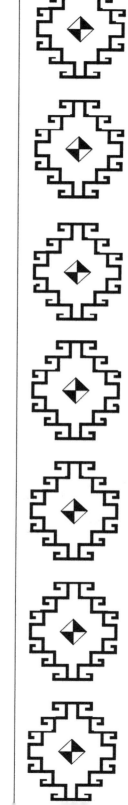

yet our third son finished a good education at Texas A & M and is now driving a taxi in New York! Why, you ask? Who knows. He majored in computer science. He says he cannot find a really good job and that taxi driving is fun. Plus, he has met a lot of people in the Indian community in New York and actually has his first Indian girlfriend. Maybe she will make him see some sense!

Life goes on, as the television show says. Our youngest daughter will leave for college soon. Except for the crazy taxi driver, all of our children are in Texas. I guess you could say I think of this as home, but then again I don't really know. America is my third country. Maybe it is best not to be too attached to a place. I see so much violence over territory here, in India, all over the world. So, yes, Texas is my home, and I welcome everyone.

PART II

In the United States

= 4 =

Prejudices and Opportunities

The Bellingham Riots

In 1907, Asian Indian workers began pouring into the logging town of Bellingham, Washington, north of Seattle. They came looking for work at the sawmills that would pay them just over two dollars a day. The mill owners welcomed them with open arms because they could pay the Punjabis less than the unionized European Americans required. Plus, the Indians had a reputation for working long, hard hours with little complaining.

Bellingham was a boom town, connected to the rest of the United States by the Great Northern Railway, on which salmon, coal, and timber were shipped. Bellingham had a history of strained race relations; mobs had driven Chinese immigrants out twenty years earlier, and Japanese immigrants were greeted a few years later with a hostile reception.

Because Sikhs were required to wear turbans and other conspicuous signs of their religion, most of the Asian Indians in Bellingham couldn't hide their origins. But mill owners had no problem employing them until anti-Indian movements were started by the unions, to which the Asian Indians did not belong.

On Labor Day (September 2, 1907), union representatives warned the mill owners to against employing the Asian Indians.

When the immigrants went to work the next day, violence erupted. Their homes were burned and some of them were assaulted. The next day, several hundred white mill workers gathered to demand that the Asian Indians leave Bellingham.

The police arrested two people but were forced to release them when it became clear that they had no power against the mob of unionized mill workers. Once the mob realized this, they stormed to the waterfront, where the Asian Indians lived, throwing them into the streets and starting a riot.

The mayor supported the Indians, and tried to protect 200 of them from the mob by keeping them in a holding cell. But the City Council, while denouncing the violence, backed the ejection of the Indians. The Bellingham Herald editorialized that an Indian "is not a good citizen. It would require centuries to assimilate him, and this country need not take the trouble."

By September 17, as many as 1,000 Asian Indians had fled Bellingham, some heading back to Canada and some moving south to work on railroad construction in California. But even those trying to flee faced obstacles. Some Indians trying to board steamships in Seattle were forced off, while others were beaten.

The Move to Keep Asian Indians Out

In November following the Bellingham riots, similar violence occurred in Everett and Danville, Washington. Asian Indians hired by the railroad in California also faced anti-Indian resistance. But it was specific laws aimed at Indians and other Asian immigrants that finally cut off Asian Indian immigration.

In 1913, primarily to bar Japanese from owning land, the California legislature passed the Alien Land Law. The statute specified that only those who were eligible for U.S. citizenship could own land in California. For Sikh farmers who had saved their money to buy land, this law was devastating.

According to a 1790 law, only "free white persons" could be naturalized, and the only amendment to that law was made after the Civil War, when ex-slaves were granted the right of citizenship. Though the decision in a 1910 case in the Court of Appeals determined that Asian Indians were indeed Caucasians, most Indian immigrants were reluctant to challenge local politicians who claimed that they were not. Buying land in California was next to impossible for the dark-skinned Punjabis.

Californians were becoming increasingly hostile to Asian immigrants. They would talk of the "Hindoo invasion" (ignorant of the fact that most of their Indian neighbors were Sikh, not Hindu) and warn against the "tide of turbans" overrunning the state. The Asiatic Exclusion League, organized to turn public opinion against all Asians in California, targeted the Indians working around the state in agriculture and railroad construction.

By 1917, anti-Asian sentiment had reached such heights that the U.S. government passed the Immigration Act of 1917. That law created, among other restrictions on immigration into the United States, a "barred zone" from which immigration was prohibited. The zone included India, Burma, Siam, and other parts of Asia (the Chinese were already excluded by an 1882 law and the Japanese and Koreans had agreed to limit emigration from their countries in 1907). Immigration from India was essentially cut off.

The United States v. Bhagat Singh Thind

But the discrimination against Asian Indians did not end there. In 1923, a landmark Supreme Court decision changed the lives of every Asian Indian American. Bhagat Singh Thind, who had served in the army during World War I, became a citizen under a federal law that allows honorably discharged veterans to be naturalized. The U.S. government tried to revoke his citizenship, arguing that he was ineligible because he wasn't white. The government used the Immigration Act of 1917's "barred zone" as an indicator that Asian Indians weren't Caucasian. U.S. v. Thind went all the way to the Supreme Court, which in 1923 ruled that Asian Indians were not eligible to be naturalized.

The previous federal decisions allowing citizenship had been based on the argument that Asian Indians were Caucasian, descending from Aryans like northern Europeans. But the Court determined that the wording of the 1790 law was intentionally nonscientific, meant to be interpreted as a determination of color, not race.

The decision read, "It may be true that the blond Scandinavian and the brown Hindu have a common ancestor in the dim reaches of antiquity, but the average man knows perfectly well that there are unmistakable and profound differences between them today." The decision went on to argue that "Caucasian" is a

Indira Ghandi was Prime Minister of India from 1966 to 1977 and again from 1980 until she was killed by her Sikh security guards in 1984. Her death sparked hatred and violence against the Sikhs all over India.

scientific term that the framers of the 1790 law didn't even know and certainly didn't intend to be applied when determining the meaning of "white person." Thind's citizenship was revoked.

Following the Thind decision, the citizenship of about 50 naturalized Asian Indians was taken away as well, until another court decision stopped the government from reversing any more naturalizations. In addition, land owned by Asian Indians was subject to confiscation by the state under the 1913 Alien Land Law. At the same time, Asian Indians in California and other western states were barred from marrying white women under antimiscegenation laws, which prohibited marriages between whites and other races. In the wake of the Thind decision, many Asian Indians returned to India. Some went voluntarily, but thousands were deported after a 1924 law outlawed the immigration of anyone not eligible for citizenship.

The Marriage Solution

One of the most devastating results of the 1917 and 1924 acts was their effect on the family life of the Sikh immigrants. Almost all of the earliest Asian Indian immigrants were men who traveled to the United States without their wives. Women were not expected to emigrate because the men thought they would be gone only temporarily. Consequently, when laws barring the immigration of Asian Indians went into effect, none of the wives could join their husbands. And if the bachelors tried to return to India and find wives, they would not be allowed back in the United States.

continued on page 69

65

Sheila Patel
Rivers All Over the World

Sheila Patel is 10 years old and lives in Hoboken, New Jersey.

I was born here in Hoboken and I have never been to India. But I know a lot about it, probably because I live around people like my parents, who are from India. I would like to visit one day, just to see my grandparents and all. Mostly I like it here. I don't think I could live somewhere that I couldn't eat pizza and hamburgers whenever I wanted. My aunt says that is a selfish thing to say. My mother says I'll see things differently one day. Who knows?

It's kind of hard to talk about myself. I mean, I'm just a kid. I have friends in school that I really like. Who are they? Just kids, you know. Some are Indian and some are—what would you call them?—just from here. We all pretty much like the same things. We think the Mighty Ducks are great! Haven't you seen those movies? Well, we've seen them a bunch of times. Most of us have Mighty Duck shirts and caps. We want to start a street hockey club, but our parents won't let us get Rollerblades yet. They think it's too dangerous for girls to be running around like that. It would be cool, though.

Of course I think about being Asian Indian. My mom wears a sari and we have Indian food most nights. We have a shrine in our house, and we burn incense every day. That is not real American, I suppose. But I like those things. Still, I don't want to dress like my mom and she doesn't make me. I don't want to when I grow up either because people look at you kind of funny. Especially when it's a holy time and she paints a bindi on her forehead. It scares me. My friend Alana told me that a few years ago there were gangs in New Jersey called "Dotbusters". They wanted to beat

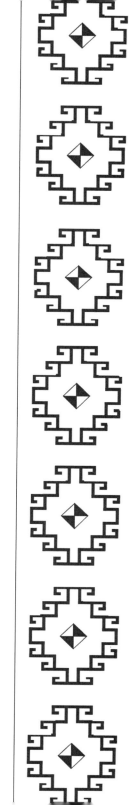

up on Indians, especially those who wore the red circle on their foreheads. My mom said that was then and things have changed, but I still worry. I hear the things people say sometimes. Like what? Like, "Go home, Hindu." I want to say I am home, but I just pretend I don't hear them. It doesn't happen that much. It's all right, really.

My mother thinks I worry about everything too much. I really am not as selfish as my aunt thinks I am. I mostly worry about the environment. I can't stand to see pictures on television of the birds and fish dying when there is an oil spill. Or those satellite photos of the forests being destroyed. It upsets me a lot. I sit in front of the altar every night before I go to bed. I don't exactly pray like you probably would. I just say the names of things that I want to be protected. I start out with the earth, the trees, the air, the water, the animals, the birds. Then I name rivers. I really like to think about rivers, so I have a long list of rivers I name. I kind of think that when I name the river the spirit of that river hears me and blesses it. Something like that. I name rivers all over the world. I just light some incense and a candle and name things. I do it silently. I sleep better afterwards.

What do I want to do? I'm not sure yet. My dad has a lot of degrees, but when he came here he couldn't find good work. He runs two newsstands and an Indian gro-cery in New York City. My two older brothers help him on weekends plus he has regu-lar employees. I think he makes pretty good money because he doesn't complain too much about it. My mother and my aunt run a day care center down the street. Many Indian women do not want to leave their children but feel better if they leave them with other Indians. I think my mother was a teacher in India. I'm not sure. That was before I was born.

My mother and father both talk about going back to India one day. I hope they don't because I don't want to go. They said it will be after I am older but I still don't

want them to leave. I am not going to go. I like it here. I will probably leave New Jersey and move to where there are more rivers and mountains, maybe somewhere in the west. Mother says maybe I will be an environmental scientist. Maybe I will, but I don't know exactly what an environmental scientist does, so I can't say yet for sure that's what I want to do.

Right now I just want to do good in school and have fun with my friends and maybe have a boyfriend. Mother says life will get complicated enough one day, so just enjoy things as best I can now.

About half the Sikh men were already married to women they left in Punjab, but among the remaining bachelors, many married Mexican women living in California. For some, this solved two problems. First, they could marry. Although Mexican women were considered white, and marriages between them and Asian Indians would technically have been prohibited, the county clerks usually looked the other way when granting marriage licenses to Indians and Mexicans. Mexican immigrants were not much more respected than Asian Indians. Second, since the Mexican women were white, they could become citizens and own land in California. Most of the Sikh men who married Mexicans would register their land in the names of their wives or their American-born children.

But the Indian-Mexican marriages were often difficult alliances. The husband was usually forced to accept that his children would have Spanish names and would be more likely to speak Spanish or English at home than Punjabi. The children were brought up in the Mexican American traditions, including the Roman Catholic religion, because there was a more established Mexican community in California. And the Sikh men found themselves confronted by wives who were more independent and attached to their circle of female friends than their counterparts in India were. Many Sikh-Mexican marriages ended in divorce.

The presence of many Sikh "uncles," the other Asian Indian men who lived without families in California, maintained some of the Indian culture within a strong Mexican American society. But it wasn't until the U.S. government lifted the ban on Asian Indian immigration and naturalization that the pockets of Sikh culture in California had the opportunity to thrive again.

The Fight for Citizenship and Equal Immigration Rights

During World War II, India, still part of the British Empire, was vital to the triumph of the Allied forces. If the Japanese were to move westward to meet up with the Germans, they would most likely come through India and try to take advantage of Indian opposition to British rule. American strategists began pushing for a congressional bill that would allow Asian Indians to immigrate with a small quota. They also pointed out that the same racist ideology behind Adolf Hitler's Nazi Party formed the basis of the argument against Asian Indian citizenship.

By 1946, Congress had passed a law permitting naturalization and a small annual immigration quota of 100 for Asian Indians. Between 1946 and 1965, however, 12,000 Asian Indians immigrated to the United States, many of them the long lost wives and families of the Sikhs in California who were not subject to the quota. And between 1947 and 1965, almost 1,800 Asian Indians became U.S. citizens. Some of them had American wives and American children but had waited years for their own chance at citizenship.

The quota of 100 was determined by a 20-year-old immigration law passed in 1924. Reacting to the enormous numbers of immigrants around the turn of the century (the period of heaviest immigration to this day) from areas other than northern Europe, Congress gave each country a quota based on 2 percent of its population in the United States at the time of the 1890 census. This system benefited northern European countries and handi-

capped countries who had not sent immigrants until after the
turn of the century.

The disadvantages of the new quotas, of course, were that
any Asian Indian not related to a citizen or permanent resident of
the United States had very little chance of immigrating to this
country, while certain European countries enjoyed quotas in the
thousands. Congress waited another 20 years before recognizing
this inequality and tried to remedy the situation by eliminating
uneven quotas with the 1965 immigration act.

However, the 1965 act included a safety measure against the
immigration of too many economically disadvantaged foreigners by
creating preference categories and awarding only a small quota to
nonpreference immigrants. The government worried that completely open immigration would draw too many people who would
end up on the rolls of the U.S. welfare system. Congress never
envisioned the number of immigrants who would still manage to
skirt the preference requirements and immigrate under family-
preference or nonpreference visas. In fact, supporters of the 1965
act, answering some representatives' fears about the number of
Asians who would pour into the country, assured Congress that
immigration would indeed increase for a few years and then trail
off steadily. They grossly miscalculated. Immigration increased
every year for the next two-and-a-half decades.

Observing the lopsided numbers of immigrants from devel-
oping countries versus those from wealthier countries,
Congress again tried to control the current by passing a law in
1990 that essentially ended immigration in nonpreference categories and significantly reduced immigration through family-
preference categories.

Fortunately for some Asian Indians, their superior education makes them prime candidates for immigration under preference visas, but these people represent only a fraction of the ballooning population of India. The vast majority of the Asian Indian people—the poor, uneducated, and unskilled—cannot escape the conditions in India through emigration to the United States.

Balancing the American Family with the Indian Culture

For those who make it to the United States and choose to stay, family life takes on a new face as children grow up more American than Indian. For many parents, deciding just how much of Indian culture to pass on to their children becomes a difficult task. Some fear too much "Indianness" will hinder their children's acceptance as Americans. Others fear that by ignoring Indian traditions and culture, they will create distance between themselves and their children and break the ties of communication.

In many Asian Indian families, traditional Indian ideals held by parents clash with American values held by children. In India, children are taught that the family is more important than the individual. Indian families often live closely and in extended family units. Children are well behaved and obedient and defer to the many decisions about career and marriage that their parents make for them.

But in the United States, many children, especially of European descent, are encouraged to be independent and speak out, and they are rewarded for being able to make their own decisions. The American way of thinking is thrust full force against the Indian way, as teens try to assert their independence and discover who they are. But in India, adolescence doesn't represent a similar rite of passage, because children will, throughout their lives, have a consistent relationship of respect to their parents. There is no such thing as growing up and becoming separated from the decisions made by one's parents. The family circle is the most intimate relationship an Asian Indian has in his or her life. In the United States, some Indian teens may rebel against the authority of their first generation Asian Indian American parents.

Asian Indian American girls may discover that their parents won't allow them to date until they are much older. Some parents

Many Indian parents teach their children Indian customs so that their culture and way of dress will be preserved.

insist on adhering to the Indian tradition of arranged marriages and expect their children to accept their choice of spouse. Basically, parents want to remain more traditional, while their children want to enjoy average American teenage freedoms.

Asian Indian American parents also feel it is important to teach their children about their heritage through festivals, books, and religion. They may become more observant of religious practices so that their children can be exposed to their culture. They might teach the children about Hindu myths through children's storybooks, until the children know more about the Hindu gods than do many Hindu children in India. They will serve Indian foods at dinner, only to discover that their children would rather have a hamburger and french fries. All of these things are done with the hopes that Indian culture will not be lost in one generation of living in the United States.

In addition, Asian Indian parents can place unrealistic expectations on their children. Asian Indians are noted for their achievements—they have been recognized as part of the "model minority" of Asians, whose academic skills have been touted around the country. But Asian Indian teens who fail to live up to these standards are often considered failures not only by their families but by others who expect them, as Asians, to be top performers. The stress caused by these feelings of failure can be devastating.

The educational achievements of Asian Americans has caused resentment among non-Asians. Asians become the targets of ethnic slurs or discrimination. In March 1993, a congressman from Maryland drew massive media attention when he commented on the number of scholarships given to Asian

Americans. Referring to a list of scholarship recipients he had seen, Representative Roscoe G. Bartlett complained that only "about a third had American names" and that a large number had "Oriental names." He went on to comment that "not much over a third of [the scholarships] went to students that would represent the normal American." He later apologized, saying he should have said "European names" instead of "American names" and admitted that most of the students with Asian names were probably Americans.

The Achievements

Sometimes the preserving of Indian culture has its benefits when the aspiration for high achievement is passed along. The structure of current immigration laws means, of course, that most Asian Indians who make it to the United States have superior education and professional skills. Statistics about their achievements compared with those of other Americans prove that this is true. Asian Indians lead in almost every aspect of lifestyle, including educational level and income.

As a group, Asian Indian Americans are relatively young, the majority being under 40. Among the men, nearly two thirds are managers or professionals. In New York City alone, that figure rises to more than 90 percent, almost half of whom are engineers, doctors, and scientists. Eighty-seven percent of Asian Indian American adults have a college education, and over one fourth have high professional degrees, such as PhDs or MDs.

The high percentage of professionals among Asian Indian

continued on page 79

Ravi

Life and Healing

Ravi is 32 years old and lives in New York City. He is a physician of both Western and Ayurvedic medicine.

I came to the United States ten years ago from New Delhi. I came as a student to Boston University School of Medicine. You might think this would have made my parents happy, but it was a source of pain and despair for my father for several years. We are Brahmin. This, as you may know, is the learned caste in Hinduism. My father is a scholar of ancient texts, and he had hoped I too would carry on this long family tradition. I began as such, but one day as I was studying the Bhagavad-Gita (a collection of holy texts written 2,500 years ago), I came across this passage in the Rig Veda:

> *I move with the infinite in Nature's power*
> *I hold the fire of the soul*
> *I hold life and healing.*

After all the sacred words I had read, it was these that spoke to me. I woke in the morning thinking of these words. I knew with complete certainty that I wanted to be a doctor. My father said I had blasphemed these words. The "I" was a holy "I," not the "I" of the personal. When that failed, he said I didn't understand metaphor. But I knew all those things, and it did not change my decision. I had been chosen and I knew it.

Once I decided to come to this country to study medicine, my family acquiesced. I liked my studies immediately. Unlike many of my colleagues, I decided not to specialize but to be a general practitioner. I still cannot exactly explain why I made this decision. It was, however, the correct one.

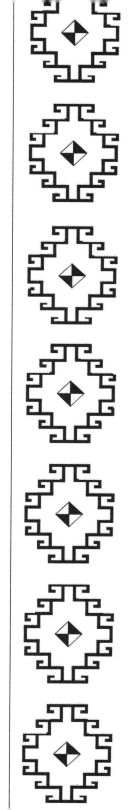

I did my residency in New York City clinics and hospitals. I still practice part time in one of the clinics where I took my residency. New York was very hard in the beginning. Not the culture, but financially. I made a small amount of money for the hard work I was doing. I think at first some patients distrusted me as their doctor. They often inquired after my English. I assured them that English was the language I was schooled in since birth so there was no cause for concern. I am often surprised at most people's lack of understanding concerning the British school system in India.

Once I began my full practice as a doctor, I had more time to consider what I was doing. I thought so often of my patients and the many problems and diseases they brought me. Many of the health problems were preventable, I was sure. So, after all this training in Western medicine, I became interested in the ancient system of healing from India—Ayurvedic medicine. I even went back to New Delhi for a time to study. The system is based on the body and emotional type of a person, and then a diet is prescribed to fit that type. It is believed that if the body is in balance, disease will not only be cured but in the future be prevented from getting the chance to take hold. I am amazed at the results. My practice now combines both types of medicine. I have a consulting practice to help people get started with the Ayurvedic way of life. I also continue my work in the clinic. I believe this new way of medicine will become more and more acceptable. Fine doctors like Deepak Chopra (who is also from New Delhi) are doing research and teaching in the United States so that more and more people are becoming interested. Dr. Chopra is becoming so well known that I believe that by the next decade people will no longer have to ask, What is Ayurvedic medicine?

I have been happy with my decision to come to America. I married last year, a fellow physician. My wife's family is from Calcutta, but she was born in this country. She is a pediatrician. We will raise our family in New York. Still, I return to India every year. I miss my family and the warmth of the culture. I even miss the way the air feels different, smells different. But with pollution the way it is now in India, no controls, those are things I might not long for anymore. And the political situation is so unstable. After Indira Gandhi was assassinated, I became obsessed with politics in my country as I never had been when I lived there. I still follow the situation closely.

But I am an American now. I can vote. My children will go to school with children of many races and countries and classes. I think this is best. The caste system in India, while no longer legal, still affects the futures of too many people. I was lucky because of it but so many people are not. I know there is hardship and poverty here, but you have seen nothing until you have seen the streets of Calcutta.

My wife and I sit before a shrine in our home every morning. We meditate silently and send blessings to our family and friends in India and in this country. When we have children, they will sit with us so that every day starts with praise. I am grateful that I followed my calling—grateful to the texts of the Bhagavad-Gita and grateful to New York.

✳ ✳ ✳

immigrants explains their relative prosperity. Their salaries on average not only exceed the national average but are higher than those of any other ethnic or racial group in the country (except Japanese Americans), including whites. The average salary of an Asian Indian American family is one and a half times the average American salary overall, and it is one hundred times the average per capita income in India. According to the 1980 census, an Asian Indian American family could expect to earn an average of $25,600 a year (including wives' salaries), whereas the average per capita income in India (where wives do not work) was about $284 a year. The latter figure, of course, averages in nonworking children and includes the salaries of uneducated and unskilled workers, but it still gives an indication of the vast difference between incomes in India and in the United States.

But high achievement is not always what it appears. Although Asian Indians are mostly professionals, they don't always find jobs in the United States that are comparable to their level of education. Even the exception to the rule, physicians, 95 percent of whom find work in their profession, often take jobs in less glamorous settings, such as inner-city hospitals, psychiatric wards, and rural clinics.

Other professionals, such as computer engineers or scientists, who are lucky enough to find good jobs in their professions, often discover that they hit a "glass ceiling." They advance in their jobs to a certain level and then cease receiving promotions. Many complain that Asians in general are perceived as technicians and are often not accepted as managers or supervisors. And though they usually receive high salaries, they tend to have more years of education than the average American earning the same wage. A

white American with the same amount of education as an Asian Indian American makes more money than his or her Asian Indian counterpart.

Receiving Minority Status

In the 1970s one group decided to fight limitations, like glass ceilings, that affect Asian Indians by lobbying for minority status for Asian Indians in the United States. The Association of Indians in America (AIA) argued for Asian Indians to be listed as a separate ethnic group in the 1980 census. In previous censuses, Asian Indians had been classified as "white/Caucasian." But the new classification would enable Asian Indians to be treated differently because of their ethnic background.

By assigning a category to Asian Indians, the government officially declared them a minority. As such, they could be eligible for affirmative action and other special concessions granted to minorities to assure equal treatment. Supporters of minority status felt that Asian Indians had certainly been the victims of discrimination. At work, they claimed, Asian Indians had been unfairly treated in hiring and firing, had received lower wages than whites, and had been denied promotions. Supporters also noted that Asian Indians had not received equal housing opportunities.

Many Asian Indians were against minority classification, citing the relative success of Asian Indian Americans among other American ethnic groups. They asserted that, except for the workplace, there were few places where Asian Indians were the victims of discrimination. In the view of the Indian League in America (ILA), special treatment for Asian Indians, particularly in the form of affirmative action while they were outperforming most Americans, might cause resentment. Some Asian Indian Americans were uncomfortable with the classification, comparing it with the caste system.

But by the 1980s, other entities were determining that some discrimination did exist. The U.S. Small Business Administration, responding to a petition filed by seven businessmen on behalf of the National Association of Americans of Asian Indian Descent, decided that Asian Indians were socially disadvantaged and therefore eligible for the agency's program to promote minority businesses. The SBA also noted that petitions it had received, signed by thousands, and accompanying comments "amply show that the group has suffered from prejudice or bias."

The "Dotbusters"

Some of that prejudice has taken the form of violence, as was clear in Jersey City and Hoboken, New Jersey, in the 1980s. The neighboring towns, just across the Hudson River from New York City, are home to a population of more than 10,000 Asian Indian Americans. In the mid-1980s, gangs were known to taunt the immigrants with verbal abuse, egg throwing, and even beatings. But in 1987, the violence reached a peak.

An Asian Indian doctor was beaten with a baseball bat and left for dead in September of that year. He suffered permanent neurological damage. That same month, Navroz Mody was beaten to death by a gang of teens who shouted "Hindu, Hindu" as they hit

him. A group calling itself the "Dotbusters"—a reference to the bindi, a red dot that some Indian women wear on their foreheads as a sign of sanctity—took responsibility for the attack. The group stated its intentions in a letter published in the *Jersey Journal* that read: "We will go to any extreme to get Indians to move out of Jersey City. If I am walking down the street and I see a Hindu and the setting is right, I will just hit him or her. We plan some of our extreme attacks, such as breaking windows—we use the phone book and look up the name Patel [a common Indian name]. Have you seen how many there are?"

The beatings were attributed mostly to jealousy. In Jersey City and Hoboken, a poorer working class lives alongside more affluent professionals who commute to New York City. Most of the Indians living there are relatively well-off and are resented by those who believe that Asian Indians are taking their jobs. Members of the working class also fear that gentrification will force them out of their homes to make way for professionals (including immigrants) trying to escape the high rents of New York City.

= 5 =

Lifestyles

Life on the West Coast at the Turn of the Century

Unlike the Asian Indian immigrants of today, who live among other ethnic and racial groups, the Sikh farmers who immigrated in the early 1900s lived in tight-knit, almost communal groups. They relied on their collective power not only to help them find work but also to survive as predominantly non-English-speaking foreigners.

Usually, Asian Indians would organize into labor gangs of about 50, led by the member who could speak the best English (often, a veteran of the British army). The leader would be paid more for his efforts at negotiating wages and act as a go-between for the bosses and workers. The gang would travel around, sharing expenses and chores and offering seasonal labor as a group, whether it was in agriculture—picking fruit, irrigating, planting, and harvesting—or in the railroad or logging industries.

No matter where they worked, the days were long—as much as 14 hours—and the work was hard, often requiring bending and lifting all day. Asian Indian labor gangs found themselves in constant competition with Japanese gangs. Cultural and language differences often kept these groups from working together.

Living arrangements for the laborers were cramped. They lived in camps, sleeping in tents or even out in the open. On some farms, they lived in barracks, with many men crammed into one small room. In these tight-knit gangs, cultural practices were preserved, especially eating habits. Each gang became like a family, one with many "uncles."

Eventually, some of these hard workers saved enough money to buy or lease land. Land purchase was one of the goals of the Sikh farmers. Some owned land as individuals, while others pooled their resources and became farming partners. Most of the individual owners were formerly gang leaders who had put their extra wages toward buying a few acres.

As farmers, the Punjabis grew the crops they knew best from

A group learns about steelmaking at the Ford Motor Company as part of the Indian Steel Training and Education Program put into effect in 1957.

their days farming in India. That usually meant planting rice or cotton and sometimes nuts and fruits. Again the work was difficult, but the new landowners were willing to rise early and work hard with the hopes of making a better living than was offered them in India. Unfortunately, the Alien Land Law and the Thind decision in 1923 sent most of them back to being laborers.

Politically, the Punjabis were rather quiet, even in the face of discriminatory acts. The few who were involved in politics were more concerned with the political situation in India than in the United States, participating in a small movement that took a volatile political stance in the 1910s. Critical of British rule, a few Asian Indian students and entrepreneurs recruited support among some of the Punjabi laborers for the Ghadr (mutiny) Party. The movement published a newspaper that urged immigrants to return to India and participate in a rebellion against the British. The Ghadr Party was even courted in World War I by the Germans, who wanted to help break the British stronghold in South Asia. However, arrests in India and in the United States effectively eliminated any threat by the party by 1917. For the Punjabi laborers, the important issue was surviving in the United States, not inciting a revolution in India.

The New Occupations

These days, most Asian Indian Americans are not farmers, though a few small Sikh farming communities still exist in California. Instead, Asian Indians who own businesses practice their trades behind the counters in motels, in Indian clothing or

grocery stores, or among the racks of magazines in New York City's newsstands.

There are a few industries in which Asian Indians dominate, one of which is the motel business. Asian Indian Americans own 28 percent of the nation's hotels and motels and 40 percent of the country's motels with fewer than 50 rooms. But Indians can also be found all around New York City, operating the newsstands that dot every street corner and subway platform. Newsstands are an ideal business because they require very little capital to start and the inventory is turned over every week.

These business owners usually get their start with the help of a relative, who acts as a go-between for the immigrant looking to be introduced to suppliers and other people necessary to opening a business. As new immigrants, many Asian Indian Americans

This Asian Indian man owns a large newsstand in Chicago. Many educated Asian Indian Americans start their own businesses when they find they can't get jobs in the professions for which they were trained.

continued on page 90

Sidar Bains
Sharing Stories

Sidar Bains is 37 years old. He is an engineer in Seattle, Washington.

I came here from India in 1979. I had a degree in computer science engineering and wanted a good job. I waited two years to emigrate to the United States. If I hadn't had my degree, my wait would have been much longer. I arrived in San Francisco so that I could look for work in what they call Silicon Valley. Luck came over with me, because I found a job my first week here. I worked in different companies in Silicon Valley until five years ago. I thought when I came here I would work and make much money and return to India eventually. Fate always has a plan you don't know about.

The best thing that happened in California was that I met my wife. I never imagined that I would not marry an Indian woman, but that is what happened. Ana is a beautiful woman of Italian descent. We have been married ten years now. She is pregnant with our first child. We wanted to wait until the right time to start a family. Our parents are very happy and relieved that we will finally have children. Her family accepted me right away even though I was not Catholic. They are very liberal. It is nice being a part of a big Italian family. Italians are much like Indians in that they are very family-oriented. My family found it a bit more difficult to understand why I had not married an Indian woman. But now that we have made several trips to India and they actually know Ana the person, they have come to accept her warmly.

We moved to Seattle because of Ana. She wanted to leave California and get away from the crowded Bay Area. She is a freelance writer and can live anywhere. I was worried about my job, but without cause. I have a job in an environmental engineering firm in Seattle that I like more than any job I have had. And it is so beautiful here. We take long hikes in the mountains. We travel on ferries to the islands that dot the Sound. It is good to be married to an American so that you can learn to see and feel in a new way. Or maybe that is just because she is so special.

It is not that I have left India behind me. How could you shed your own skin? As a matter of fact, I have become very interested in Asian Indian immigrants since moving to Washington. Many Sikhs came to Bellingham and Everett, Washington, at the turn of the century to log. I was surprised to learn this and also surprised to learn about how violently they were driven from this area. It made me think about my fellow Indians more, especially the ones who have lived here for a long time. I began to search out long-standing communities and talk to people. I have done this in Washington and in Northern California. I now record the stories I hear, especially from the older people.

I want to publish a book one day of all the stories. They are so rich with history and culture. I have come to realize that we exist primarily through our stories. The best way to learn and to relate to others, especially those different from ourselves, is through our stories. I don't want to think of those old people, with their knowledge and humor and pain, leaving without giving their stories to us. Ana also thinks this is a good idea. She enjoys the stories and has given them to an American editor who says that when I am ready, she will help me find a publisher.

It is hard to explain how I have become such an American yet at the same time am so deeply interested in my own culture, my own people. But it is true. And this interest has made me more aware of other immigrant groups as well. I look around Seattle and see people from Chile and Vietnam and Mexico and China. I wonder what their stories are. I am sure they are very different and yet similar to ours. I think maybe this is the best part of being an American: that we look so different and have so many great stories to tell. I mean all of us, the Europeans and the Native Americans, the African Americans and the Japanese.

Well, you can see I get very excited about this. I know I am supposed to be talking about being an Asian Indian in America. I am, in a way. Perhaps my experience is atypical because of Ana. I don't know. I just know that by listening to other people I have come to know myself as an Indian and as an American much better. Maybe that is just the secret, no? To listen.

Many Asian Indian Americans find themselves in jobs that don't reflect their level of education. This street vendor holds a university degree.

don't have the credit history or collateral they need to take out loans or prove to possible business associates that they are good risks. By being introduced through a relative already trusted by the supplier, banker, or licensing agency, an Asian Indian can speed up an otherwise much more lengthy process.

What is surprising about the new entrepreneurs is not their swiftness in getting a business started but their level of education. Most of the business owners are college graduates who have been unable to find work in their professional fields. They start their own businesses as an alternative to unemployment. As more and more Asian Indians immigrate to the United States, they will be joined by relatives who may have less education than their sponsoring family members. It is likely that the new immigrants will work in Asian-Indian owned businesses rather than as professionals. The domination of the motel and newsstand industries by Asian Indians will continue and grow, as more of the newest Asian Indian immigrants start businesses and fewer arrive with the education necessary to find professional work.

For the professionals who are able to find work in their fields, the road to success can be long. Often, foreign-educated professionals must first pass qualifying exams to be allowed to practice in the United States. Each state has different laws on professional licensing, but many require foreign graduates to take retraining or refresher courses before they can be certified in that state.

In the meantime, these Asian Indians must work somewhere. Some try to stay within their fields while waiting for certification—a physician may work in a medical lab or as an ambulance attendant, or a certified public accountant may prepare tax forms or keep the books in a company's accounting office. But many of the out-of-work professionals can be found in completely unrelated jobs. It is not unusual to find that your Asian Indian cabdriver in New York is a fully qualified engineer, or that the maître d' at the Indian restaurant has a Ph.D. in physics.

While Asian Indians as a group tend to prosper in the United States, they don't flaunt their wealth by buying a lot of expensive things. Most Asian Indians prefer to save their money and live more modestly.

Asian Indian Americans, on average, save 20 to 40 percent of their salaries, compared with 10 percent for Americans overall. They are usually saving their money to buy a home, considered an important investment and a symbol of security and family prestige. Although they avoid conspicuous displays of wealth, they will almost certainly spend any money necessary on their children's educations.

Women Change Their Lifestyles

One of the few expensive purchases Asian Indians will make is the jewelry that Indian women wear. Always made with 22-karat gold or better, the jewelry that adorns an Indian woman dressed in all her finery may have large precious stones, such as rubies, diamonds, emeralds, or sapphires. In India, the outfits of the higher caste women are considered incomplete without a lot of expensive accessories. Jewels are an indication of status and femininity. But in the United States, many Asian Indian women don't feel safe flashing expensive jewels. They put aside their best pieces and only wear them for special occasions.

It's not unusual to see an Asian Indian woman in the United States dressed in a traditional sari, an ornate cotton or silk cloth worn wrapped around the body, with a bindi adorning her fore-

head. Sikh women may appear in public dressed in an Indian tunic and trousers, and Muslim women can be seen across the country with veils covering their hair. Though their male counterparts are apt to adopt Western dress (with the exception of the turbans worn by Sikh men), Asian Indian women preserve some of their traditions regarding clothes, which often center on the celebration of a woman's beauty, morality, and role as wife and mother.

Yet the concept of traditional roles for Asian Indian women has been changing among many Indian immigrants. Most Asian Indian American women were educated in India, but often merely to make them more attractive as wives. Few women, especially married ones, work in India. But in the United States, most Asian Indian families include a working wife, necessitated by the need for two incomes to pay the bills. For many Asian Indian men,

Two fathers caring for their young children, evidence of the changes in male-female relationships among Asian Indians when they move the United States. In India, men are far less likely to help their wives with child-rearing duties.

accepting a wife's new role as partial provider takes some adjusting. But they rarely disapprove of or resent their wives' working, although the women may begin to adapt the more independent ways of American women.

Asian Indian American women hold professional jobs as well, though less often in the careers that require many years of education. While men work as engineers, managers, chemists, pharmacists, or computer scientists, women hold positions as nurses, teachers, lab technicians, secretaries, or bookkeepers. The one exception seems to be among Asian Indian American physicians, one third of whom are women. Among second-generation Asian Indian American women, however, the occupational distribution is much closer to that of their male counterparts.

Marriage and family are important considerations for an Asian Indian woman. In India, marriages are often arranged, but they tend to last longer than American marriages. Divorce is rare among Asian Indian American couples and virtually nonexistent among the Sikh members of this group. The majority of Asian Indian immigrants to the United States are married before coming here, but among those who are single, marriage quickly becomes an issue. Most Indian women are expected to marry between the ages of 18 and 22, and those who fail to marry by then may resort to matchmakers or personal ads to find a mate.

In fact, personal advertising for spouses is quite common among Asian Indian Americans, who use this system to find other Asian Indians with the same interests and values. Since arranged marriages are common in India, the advertisers may be a woman's parents or siblings, and the stigma attached by Americans to the use of "last resort" personal ads is not an issue. By placing personal ads, known as "matrimonials," Asian Indian Americans attempt to reconcile the concepts of arranged marriages, which are the norm in India, and romantic marriages, which are the norm among Americans.

Matrimonials can be found in the various Asian Indian newspapers published in the United States. Both U.S. residents and potential immigrants still in India will place the ads, stating "proffered" (offered) and "desired" attributes. The emphasis in most of the ads is on language and religion, since these are the dividing factors within Indian society. The matrimonials make few references to caste, but profession is often used as an indicator of social position. And there are many concessions to the American perception of marriage as a romantic union, with references to "appearance" and "loving and caring" mates.

Sikhism

Arranged marriages are not universal among Asian Indians. The practice is common to the Hindu majority of India, but the other religions in India have markedly different customs, which they bring with them when they immigrate to the United States. The most obvious differences can be observed among the Sikh population.

Sikhism was formed 500 years ago by Guru Nanak, a man trying to combine Hinduism and Islam, the dominant religions of South Asia. The new faith maintained the Hindu belief in reincarnation but did away with the caste system. It also incorporated the Islamic belief in only one god.

Because the structure of the Sikh religion was born out of a struggle for power between the Hindus and Muslims, the Sikh members became religious soldiers. The legacy of that struggle lives on in the religion today in the preservation of the "Five K's," which all Sikhs are required to wear. They are: kes (unshorn hair and beard), kacch (trousers to the knee, often worn as underwear), kara (bangle worn on the right wrist), kirpan (sword) or khanda (dagger), and khanga (hair comb). The unshorn hair is worn under a turban, probably the most noticeable sign of Sikhism in an Asian Indian American. In fact, special consideration has been made in the law for this religious practice by allowing Sikhs to be exempt from wearing certain safety devices on the head, like a hardhat on construction sites.

The Sikh world is largely a "man's world." Marriage is expected, and Sikhs marry young, primarily to begin the process of creating a family sooner. They believe that a man cannot enter the kingdom of heaven without having a male heir. Families may start having children early and continue until a boy is born, creating a tendency among Sikhs for large families. Divorce is almost

---

unknown among Sikhs in the United States, a surprising statistic considering they make up more than one third of the Asian Indian population in California, the state with the highest divorce rate.

Education remains an important consideration for Sikhs in the United States, and many Sikhs will get their higher education before they marry. In this male-oriented society, education is more important for the men than the women. Among Sikhs in the United States, men are expected to complete graduate work in their field, while women generally complete an undergraduate education.

The Sikh community centers on the Sikh temple, or Gurdawara (literally "house of the Guru"). Most Sikhs in the United States still live in tight-knit communities, reminiscent of the neighborhoods created by the turn-of-the-century immigrants, though association with the larger American population is becoming more common. The Gurdwara serves not only as a religious temple but also as a community center and a focal point for Sikh culture and traditions. It is also a source of political news and organization.

Many of today's Sikh immigrants are refugees from the political situation in India. It is understandable, then, that they would bring some of their political protests with them to the United States. They may use religious assemblies to distribute information about American policies concerning India, especially when the policy has an effect on the situation in the Punjab.

The Muslims

Though Sikhs made up the majority of the first Asian Indian immigrants, as many as 10 percent of the earliest were Muslims, members of the Islamic faith who created the basis for the modern

Asian Indian American Islamic population. Today, Muslims constitute a small part of the Asian Indian American community, though they are joined in the United States by Muslims from many other countries.

The religion of Islam has its origins 1,300 years ago with the prophet Muhammad. It is closely related to Judaism and Christianity, which form the basis for the history of the religion before Muhammad's birth. Muslims observe very strict rules on diet and prayer. They do not drink alcohol or eat pork, and they observe kosher laws. Between the kosher groceries operated for Jews and for the black Muslims in the United States, Asian Indian Muslims have little trouble finding the proper foods. Muslims must also pray five times a day and attend Friday evening prayer meetings. They read the Koran for spiritual guidance and are required to make a pilgrimage to Mecca, a holy city in Saudi Arabia, once before they die.

Like the Sikhs, Asian Indian Muslims combine religious worship with social and cultural gatherings in the United States. Sometimes the mosques serve not only Indian Muslims but Pakistani Muslims as well. The majority of the Muslims who lived in India before independence left in 1947 when the British territory was split. They went to Pakistan or, later, to the independent state of Bangladesh. Almost all the Muslims from these countries speak the common South Asian language of Urdu, though both Arabic and English may be used in services.

One of the benefits of immigration for Asian Indian Muslims is that they are reunited with the Muslims from Pakistan, and the two groups join to form one South Asian Islamic community in the United States. This becomes especially important when popular opinion among non-Muslim Americans turns against Islam because of the frequently volatile situation in the Middle East, where the majority of the world's Muslims live.

A Muslim man stands in front of a storefront mosque in New York City where he prays every afternoon. In the United States, Muslims make up a small percentage of Asian Indian immigrants but meet other adherents to Islam from all nationalities.

Christians, Jains, and Zoroastrians

Aside from the more prominent religions of Hinduism, Sikhism and Islam, a small minority of Asian Indian Americans are Christians, Jains, Buddhists, and Zoroastrians.

Christianity has a long history in India, dating back to the time when St. Thomas is said to have made a missionary visit to Kerala in A.D. 52, long before Christianity made its way to Europe. The Christians who now live in Kerala are known as the St. Thomas Christians, but in the United States they are affiliated with the Mar Thoma Syrian Church of Malabar or the Malankara Orthodox Diocese of America. Others belong to various parishes of the Orthodox Catholic and Roman Catholic religions. Most of these Christians came to the United States in the 1970s, when the women from Kerala, who were primarily nurses, came in response to the nursing shortage early in that decade.

Jainism is a 2,500-year-old religion that believes in the sanctity of life. It is a gentle religion, practiced by Mahatma Gandhi, that preaches that no living creature should be harmed. Not only are Jains vegetarians, but they will sweep the path in front of them so as not to step on anything living. They won't even eat root vegetables because harvesting them could be destructive to insect life. The various subgroups of this religion, the members of which come mostly from Gujerat and Maharashtra, celebrate their religion together in the United States, gathering for services and festivals.

Zoroastrians, also known as Parsis because the religion originated 2,700 years ago in the Pars area of Iran, first came to India as refugees from the Muslim conquest of Persia. Zoroastrians believe that the world is divided into forces of good and evil and that it is up to people to live by good thoughts, words, and deeds. Most of the Parsis are educated professionals in the upper classes. Their low birthrate, common among most of the world's wealthiest, threatens to extinguish the Parsi sect because they refuse to accept converts.

Hinduism

Hindus are by far the majority of Asian Indians, representing 83 percent of the population of India. In the United States their influence has been widespread, surprisingly so because Hindus were barely visible here until the 1960s.

Hinduism is a religion of many gods. Hindu religious beliefs and rules for daily life are set down in the Bhagavad-Gita, holy texts written 2,500 years ago. Reincarnation, karma, and the caste system are central to Hinduism, as are nonviolence and the sanctity of life. Home shrines are essential in Hinduism, and many Asian Indians worship primarily through individual faith and family gatherings, only rarely attending official temple services. But in the United States there is greater participation in Hindu temples as Asian Indian Americans seek to maintain an Indian cultural identity that they can pass on to their children.

There are over 100 Hindu temples and associations in the United States, concentrated in the larger cities, where a practicing Indian can often find a Brahmin to perform life-cycle and family rituals. When away from the temples, Hindu families engage in their own traditions, observing the morning and evening worships, periods of meditation, and the reading of sacred texts and prayers.

An American woman practicing the strengthening exercises of yoga. Originally a Hindu practice, yoga gained popularity in the United States in the 1960s and 1970s.

There are many sects of Hinduism in India, which eventually blend together out of necessity in the United States. A unique form of American Hindu worship is formed out of the many teachings brought here from north and south India. It is not unusual for an Americanized prayer to add names like Mississippi, Ohio, or Hudson to the names of the Sacred Rivers.

While American life has had an effect on the practice of Hinduism in the United States, Hinduism has also influenced American life, especially through the introduction of ayurveda, yoga, and transcendental meditation (TM). TM came to the United States in 1959 with the Maharishi Mahesh Yogi. It involves sitting and repeating a verbal incantation, called a mantra, in an attempt to achieve spiritual and physical relaxation.

Americans have recently recognized TM, along with yoga, a system of exercises that strengthens the body and focuses the mind, as restful and healthy. During the 1960s and 1970s, these practices gained popularity among Americans as they watched celebrities like the Beatles join in the craze for a new form of relaxation, exercise, and inner cleansing. Today, yoga classes can be found on almost every health club's exercise schedule, and millions of Americans dabble occasionally in meditation without realizing its Indian origins.

Ayurveda, a medical science that emphasizes a physical, mental, and spiritual balance, uses medication, diet, yoga, and meditation to cure illness and achieve healthfulness. Though practiced by Asian Indian Americans since their arrival here, ayurveda has gained considerable respect among other Americans who seek alternative medicines.

Indian Decor, Food, and Festivals

Aside from the presence in the United States of yoga and meditation, Asian Indians have brought some of their other cultural elements into this country. Indian textiles and foods can be found in homes all across the United States.

Indian batiks have become extremely popular in American decor in recent years. These ornately designed textiles are made by dying fabrics on which wax has been applied to create a decorative pattern. Traditional Indian batik designs become wall hangings, pillow covers, and even clothes. Many ornately dyed shirts and loose pants have patterns that not only originated in India but are still produced there as well, and then imported and sold by Asian Indian Americans.

Indian food is also making its way into the American home.

continued on page 106

Imrat Chagla
Best of Both Worlds

Imrat Chagla is 22 years old and lives in Oakland, California. He works doing data entry and studies the tablas.

I was 5 when I came to this country with my parents. My father is a doctor with the Kaiser Medical Centers and my mother is a nurse in the AIDS ward at the University of California Medical Center. I was growing up pretty normal in San Francisco, thinking about being a doctor, when my father took me to a performance of the tablas in Golden Gate Park. I was 12. I have not wanted to do anything else since that time. From what I hear, it often happens that way with the tablas.

What are the tablas? You don't know? Well, I understand. I didn't know either until that concert. I'd probably heard them in music, but, you know, didn't really get what they were. They are drums that you play with your hands, not sticks. It is an ancient art form in India. You have to study with a master to learn and it is very demanding. My father resisted until I was 15. I finally promised to go to college no matter what my intentions with the tablas. So he let me begin to study.

It is difficult to explain the tablas. You must learn so many patterns and rhythms and in the correct order. There are speech syllables to learn with each separate "song." This is good because you can practice even without the tablas, driving to lessons, in the shower. But nothing compares with the drums themselves. They are usually accompanied with a sitar or similar string instrument. Oh, the concerts can go on all night! You enter into another world with the tablas.

I did go to college at the University of California at Berkeley. I majored in biology so my father could feel I might still be a doctor. I minored in history so I could try and figure out the world. I know, I'm young that way. Anyway, I studied the tablas the whole time. I met so many people this way. Not just fellow Indians but American musicians who wanted to know the mysteries. There are two very revered tabla players from India in the Bay Area, and I

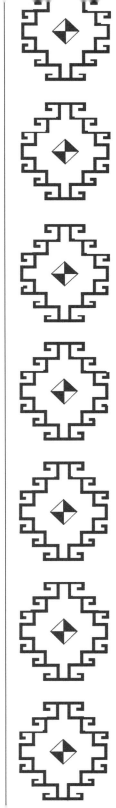

have studied with both: Swapan Chandhuri and Zakir Hussain. If you ever have a chance to go to a concert to hear either of them, go and it will explain everything I have tried to tell you.

Okay. I'm not making a living this way. I have a part-time job doing data entry. I really don't mind because at least it helps keep my fingers strong. My father is beginning to feel some pride in my music, I think, especially since my sister has decided to go to medical school. She really took the pressure off me. I am giving a small concert soon and my family will be there. I'm very excited.

I guess you can tell that I am happy that my parents moved here from India. It often seems to me that I have the best of both worlds. I have some of the traditions of India, but I also have the chance to live a different sort of life here. My cousins in India are having trouble finding work, and many of them are trying to come and be with us. Besides, there is so much political and religious strife in India now that we have not even returned for almost ten years.

I have had some problems with ethnic slurs, but not too many. It is usually when I leave the Bay Area. It is pretty diverse and accepting here. Once I was traveling north of Redding, California, and stopped with a friend at a restaurant to eat lunch. When I came out, someone had painted "Hindu" on my car. It not only angered me, but it was stupid, too. You would think people in the United States would be smarter than that. I mean, not everyone from India is a Hindu. Hinduism is a religion, not a race. I'm Christian, actually. My entire family has been Christian for generations. But they see you and they think, "Hindu." I feel fine about the religion Hinduism, but I just know what they are trying to say by using that term. It is a mean and ignorant thing to do.

I don't know what is going to happen with me and my music career. I play sometimes with a band that does world music and use my tablas to make dance music. It's okay. I like the band members and some of the music. But nothing compares to the pure ancient form of tabla. I'm young still and ready for what will happen. So, I'm just going to keep doing what I do. I have a good family and friends. I guess you could say I'm just kind of a regular American guy in many ways. Except for this tabla thing!

Though still considered exotic, sauces flavored with curry, corian-der, or saffron are becoming popular, and vegetarian dishes cooked in American restaurants often have an Indian origin. Indian restaurants, serving anything from tandoori chicken and naan (a flat Indian bread) to dishes cooked in the spicy vindaloo style and appetizers with paneer cheese, are easy to find in the larger cities.

But American styles of eating have influenced Asian Indians in return. Most Asian Indians are vegetarians or have strict eating habits as a rule of their religions. Among Hindus, a taboo against killing or causing bodily harm to any living being for food or other purposes prevents them from eating meat. Cattle, especially, are sacred to Hindus. Jains, of course, adhere to a strict vegetarian diet, and though Sikhism has no religious restrictions on meat eat-ing, most Sikhs are vegetarians as well. Muslims follow kosher laws and cannot eat pork. Almost all Asian Indians abstain from drinking alcohol, except the lower castes and the very wealthy. But in the United States many of these eating habits change.

Some Hindus and Sikhs eventually start eating eggs and fish, and then move on to white meats like chicken and pork. It is not unusual for them to start eating beef, at first unknowingly—because no one has told them what's in the hamburger they are eating—and eventually knowingly. The conversion from vegetarian to meat eater can take many years, and a lot of Asian Indians never give in to the American love for meat, but the conversion sometimes comes from sheer necessity in a country that puts little emphasis on making vegetarian meals accessible. Muslims, on the other hand, tend to stick more closely to their religious restric-tions because of the resources available to them through black Muslim kosher groceries.

Many Asian Indians eat at least a portion of their meals American-style. At least half of Asian Indians eventually start eating a typical American breakfast of cereal or toast and coffee or even eggs rather than the richer Indian breakfast, which can resemble an American dinner with rice and meat and heavy sauces. They also tend to eat the standard American sandwich lunch. It is dinner that they reserve as the one meal in which Indian food is served, consisting of a full course meal of rice, bread, vegetables, salad, and sometimes meat, seasoned with cumin, curry, tumeric, coriander, basil, peppers, and other Indian spices. But many Asian Indian parents find that their second-generation Asian Indian American children prefer American food, and dinner may soon end up to be pizza, burgers, or macaroni and cheese.

This Indian restaurant is located on East 6th Street in Manhattan, a street that is famous for its live Indian music, curries, and breads.

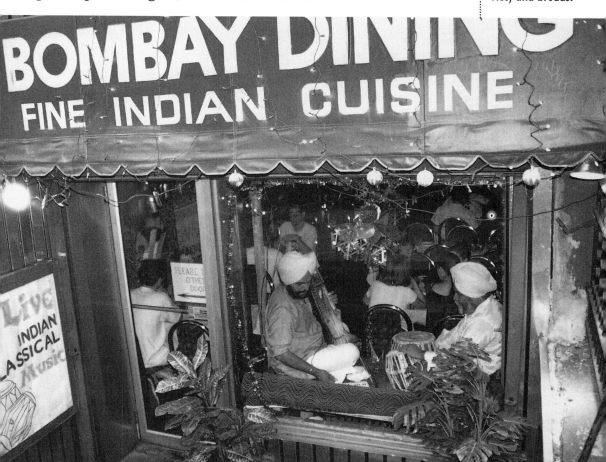

Dinner is served rather late, in the Indian style. This habit comes from the custom of serving a light meal in the late afternoon, derived from the British teatime. Many Asian Indians still have their tea at 4 o'clock, complete with snacks. Indians drink a lot of tea in general and less coffee. Alcoholic beverages become part of the Asian Indian American diet as well, though more for men than for women, and never for Muslims.

Though American foods have crept into the Asian Indian American diet, traditional foods continue to be central to the many Indian celebrations that are still observed in the United States. The Hindu festivals of Diwali (the Indian New Year and the festival of lights, celebrated in September or October) and Basant Panchimi (the celebration of the coming of spring), as well as numerous other Hindu celebrations, are observed by Asian Indian Americans. Muslims observe the holy month of Ramadan, in which fasting is practiced from dawn to sunset. Sikhs use various religious festivals as occasions to maintain social contacts, the most important of which is the celebration of the birthday of Guru Nanak.

As Asian Indians continue to come to the United States, their traditions and festivals will become more prominent in cities and towns across the nation. As the fastest-growing Asian minority in the country, Asian Indian Americans are to an increasing degree exerting an influence over the everyday culture of the United States and raising the standards of education, profession, and family values among all Americans.

For Further Reading

Dasgupta, Sathi Sengupta. *On the Trail of an Uncertain Dream: Indian Immigrant Experience in America.* New York: AMS Press, 1989.

Gordon, Susan. *Asian Indians.* New York: Franklin Watts, 1990.

Jensen, Joan M. *Passage from India: Asian Indian Immigrants in North America.* New Haven: Yale University Press, 1988.

Melendy, Howard Brett. *Asians in America: Filipino, Koreans, and East Indians.* New York: Hippocrene Books, 1981.

Mukerji, Dhan Gopal. *Caste and Outcast.* New York: E. P. Dutton, 1923.

Saran, Parmatma. *The Asian Indian Experience in the United States.* New Delhi: Vikas, 1985.

_, ed. *The New Ethnics: Asian Indians in the United States.* New York: Praeger, 1980.

Takaki, Ronald. *Strangers from a Different Shore: A History of Asian Americans.* Boston: Little, Brown, 1989.

Williams, Raymond Brady. *Religions of Immigrants from India and Pakistan: New Threads in the American Tapestry.* New York: Cambridge University Press, 1988.

Index